ALL T[...]

"A 21-gun salute for [...], original, authentic mi[...] pounding finale."

—Carolyn Hart, Pulitzer Prize–[...] [...]or of the bestselling Death on Demand series

"*All the Wrong Moves* has all the right stuff . . . Fast-paced adventure starring an irreverent heroine you'll never forget. I couldn't put it down!"

—Vicki Lewis Thompson, *New York Times* bestselling author

"Samantha is great—sassy and indomitable and believable . . . [The] action never stops."

—Joanna Carl, author of the bestselling Chocoholic Mysteries

"Well paced, this chatty first-person narrative develops the character of the not-so-military-type heroine who doesn't deal well with authority figures but does the best she can because she knows her job's important. Crime fans will look forward to Lt. Spade's next adventure."

—*Publishers Weekly*

"What fun! Merline Lovelace delivers a wisecracking heroine with a fascinating and interesting occupation that teams her with a cast of eccentric and peculiar characters. If you are looking for a good laugh with a strong mystery, *All the Wrong Moves* is the perfect choice."

—*Fresh Fiction*

"Merline Lovelace's new novel, *All the Wrong Moves*, is a great start to a new mystery series. I enjoyed her fast-paced first-person narrative, and I like United States Air Force Lieutenant Samantha Spade a lot."

—*INDenverTimes*

continued . . .

CATCH HER IF YOU CAN

MERLINE LOVELACE

BERKLEY PRIME CRIME, NEW YORK

THE BERKLEY PUBLISHING GROUP
Published by the Penguin Group
Penguin Group (USA) Inc.
375 Hudson Street, New York, New York 10014, USA
Penguin Group (Canada), 90 Eglinton Avenue East, Suite 700, Toronto, Ontario M4P 2Y3, Canada
(a division of Pearson Penguin Canada Inc.)
Penguin Books Ltd., 80 Strand, London WC2R 0RL, England
Penguin Group Ireland, 25 St. Stephen's Green, Dublin 2, Ireland (a division of Penguin Books Ltd.)
Penguin Group (Australia), 250 Camberwell Road, Camberwell, Victoria 3124, Australia
(a division of Pearson Australia Group Pty. Ltd.)
Penguin Books India Pvt. Ltd., 11 Community Centre, Panchsheel Park, New Delhi—110 017, India
Penguin Group (NZ), 67 Apollo Drive, Rosedale, North Shore 0632, New Zealand
(a division of Pearson New Zealand Ltd.)
Penguin Books (South Africa) (Pty.) Ltd., 24 Sturdee Avenue, Rosebank, Johannesburg 2196,
South Africa

Penguin Books Ltd., Registered Offices: 80 Strand, London WC2R 0RL, England

CATCH HER IF YOU CAN

A Berkley Prime Crime Book / published by arrangement with the author

PRINTING HISTORY
Berkley Prime Crime mass-market edition / January 2011

Copyright © 2011 by Merline Lovelace.
Cover illustration by Michael Gibbs.
Cover design by Rita Frangie.
Interior text design by Kristin del Rosario.

ISBN: 978-0-425-23925-4

BERKLEY® PRIME CRIME
Berkley Prime Crime Books are published by The Berkley Publishing Group,
a division of Penguin Group (USA) Inc.,
375 Hudson Street, New York, New York 10014.
BERKLEY® PRIME CRIME and the PRIME CRIME logo are trademarks of Penguin Group (USA) Inc.

PRINTED IN THE UNITED STATES OF AMERICA

10 9 8 7 6 5 4 3 2 1

To my own handsome hero, Al.
Thanks for all the grand adventures!

CHAPTER ONE

I was at Pancho's bar/cafe/motel/convenience store when I lifted the lid on a dented beer cooler and discovered three severed heads. Or more precisely, I was in the dirt parking lot outside Pancho's bar/cafe/etc., trying without success to get Snoopy SNFIR to heel. Or sit. Or just *puh-leese* stop crawling all over everything!

I admit I was pretty exasperated at that point. Sergeant Cassidy and I had chased the little robot across the desert for close to five hours that May afternoon. I was hot and sweaty and really, really looking forward to a cool one before beginning the return trip to our remote test site.

Before going into the gory details of what happened next, I guess I should introduce myself. I'm Samantha. Samantha JoEllen Spade, former cocktail waitress at the Paris casino in Las Vegas. Through a convoluted set of circumstances involving my jerk of an ex-husband and our over-endowed tramp of a neighbor, I traded the bright lights and big tippers of Sin City for a commission as a second lieutenant in the United States Air Force.

I'm sure there have been more troublesome second lieutenants in the long and storied history of the military. You wouldn't think so, though, if you'd heard my boss at the Air Force Research Lab when he announced that he'd arranged a "career broadening" assignment for me to the Defense Advanced Research Projects Agency. That's DARPA in military lingo. For reasons I've yet to comprehend during my twenty-two months in uniform, the military never uses whole words if they can possibly avoid them. I've learned to string whole sentences together using only initials. Lest you think I'm exaggerating, check out the DOD DMAT, aka the Department of Defense Dictionary of Military and Associated Terms. It's available online in PDF format and runs to a mere 780 pages!

But I digress. As mentioned above, I was "loaned" to DARPA as a brand-new second looey. The agency's mission is to develop far-out technologies that could improve the war-fighting capabilities of our military services. It does that through program managers who loll around in nice, air-conditioned offices in Arlington, Virginia, and shovel out big bucks to universities and high-powered research centers across the country.

Wish to heck I was one of those fat-cat program managers. No such luck. My reputation must have preceded me, as I was treated to a brief orientation at DARPA headquarters before being shipped out to El Paso, Texas, as OIC of FST-3. (See what I mean about initializing! It's a disgusting habit but as infectious as pinkeye.) What I *meant* to say is that I was designated officer in charge of Future Systems Test Cadre—Three.

FST-3's mission—and that of its two sister cadres— is to evaluate projects that don't meet headquarters' threshold for direct oversight. Translation: we play with inventions submitted by mom-and-pop enterprises, retired high school chemistry teachers, and pimply adolescents who like to tinker with devices that weren't designed to be tinkered with.

FST-1 is based in Alaska and tests items with potential for cold weather application. FST-2 does its thing in the Florida Everglades. Our venue is desert terrain. Hence the hot, bumpy chase Sergeant Cassidy and I had just made through twenty-plus miles of cactus-infested terrain.

A few words about Staff Sergeant Noel Cassidy. He's six-three, steely-eyed, and keeps his hair buzzed so near to his scalp that he looks bald. A Special Ops type with several combat tours and a bunch of years of service under his belt, Noel got shuffled off to FST-3 after an unfortunate misunderstanding with an undercover vice cop.

The experience did a real number on his muscle-bound psyche. The poor guy has yet to recover from the shock of learning that he got turned on by a cop in drag. Just between you and me, though, it's taking Noel a loooong time to sort through his issues. But when I mentioned as much to his military shrink, she merely smoothed her honey-colored bob and treated me to a bland smile. Since then I've tried *very* hard not to think about Sergeant Cassidy's extended sessions on her couch.

The third player in this little drama with its head still attached is a robot. He was created from spare parts and Radio Shack circuitry by Allen H. Farnsworth, an Iowa potato farmer and self-proclaimed renewable-energy nut. Farmer Farnsworth labeled his creation Self-Nurturing Find and Identify Robot—SNFIR for short. According to Farnsworth's passionate letter requesting FST-3's evaluation, his little thingamajig could sniff out, extract, and chow down on naturally occurring biodegradable energy sources like twigs and grass and garbage, thus providing itself a limitless fuel supply.

The concept caught my team's interest. We're suckers for gizmos and gadgets with even the slightest potential for military application. This one definitely had that. If it worked, SNFIR could travel indefinitely to scope out enemy territory. Or scoot ahead of Humvees to sniff out IEDs. Or provide a platform to ferry munitions to pinned-down troops. Or transport wounded back behind the lines.

Pretty grandiose hopes for an invention that, when it arrived at our test site, my team instantly dubbed Snoopy. As in Snoopy Sniffer. Remember him? The toy dog with droopy ears you pulled around on a string?

Not that I ever played with one. Girly girl that I am, I preferred Barbie dolls to clacking hounds. But I remember one of my brothers smacking a cousin in the mouth with the wooden toy and knocking out two teeth. The same brother, by the way, who's now on his fourth wife and trying to make it as an Ultimate Extreme Wrestler. What does that tell you about the collection of losers and boozers who comprise my family?

Back to SNFIR. He really does resemble the wooden Snoopy of old. His torso is about the size of a shoebox mounted on toy tractor wheels. A sort of elongated snout with imbedded sensors sniffs out organic materials. When the sensors find something yummy, a mechanical arm with a claw at the end rises out of the robot's back to scoop up the munchies. You know the kind of claw I'm talking about. You see them in those machines kids feed three or four dollars' worth of quarters into hoping to latch onto a stuffed frog, only to end up with five cents' worth of bubble gum. Instead of candy or stuffed animals, Snoopy's claw scooped up rotting vegetation and dumped it into his built-in fuel processor.

That was without the plastic ears and bobbing wire tail one of my wiseass team members glued onto the little robot. *With* them, you'd swear you could hook him on a leash on and take him out for a walk in the park, properly armed with a pooper-scooper, of course.

Except this Snoopy doesn't need to be leashed. Guided by GPS and preprogrammed instructions, he chugs along on his tractor wheels like the Little Engine That Could. Over dry humps of earth. Around prickly cacti. Down into and up out of steep arroyos. Every so often he stops to check out a fuel source and feed himself.

When Sergeant Cassidy and I took ole Snoop out for this field test, we got a kick out of the little critter. At first. Following along on ATVs, we'd grinned at his flapping ears and traded jokes whenever he'd stopped to sniff out a snack. Then the arm would emerge from his back, the claw would snap its jaws, and twigs or decaying plant matter would disappear into his external combustible engine. After digesting his meal, Snoop would huff on.

My grin fell off my face, however, when he chugged up to the bloated carcass of banner-tailed kangaroo rat. I knew it was a banner tail because one of the members of my team is a double PhD who drives the rest of us nuts with her lengthy discourses on the flora and fauna of the north Chihuahuan Desert. I've learned to smile and tune her out once she gets started, but enough useless detail seeps into my subconscious to pop up at unexpected moments.

Like this one.

As Snoopy's arm came up with the disgusting mess in its claw, I brought my ATV to a skittering halt and jerked my radio off my belt.

"O'Reilly! This is Spade. Come in, please."

"Yo," my team's software guru drawled. "Speak to me, oh, Goddess of Gadgets."

Dennis O'Reilly isn't real big on military protocol. Neither am I, for that matter, although I have exercised my somewhat dubious authority as team chief to censor some of his more colorful titles.

"I thought you reviewed Snoopy's code," I said, scrunching my face in disgust as the kangaroo rat's gory remains disappeared into the hopper.

"I did."

"When you confirmed he was programmed to detect,

identify, and consume a wide variety of energy sources, did you know that included, like, dead rodents?"

"I did."

"And you didn't deem it advisable to share that information with me?"

"I did," he said again, with noticeable sarcasm this time. "As a matter of fact, I highlighted a few of the juicier items in the appendix of potential fuel sources that Farmer Farnsworth sent with Snoop. You read it, didn't you?"

The question was purely rhetorical. I knew it. Dennis knew it. The damned appendix had run to more than sixty pages.

"I may not have read the *entire* list," I conceded, "but I did read the specs. You can program Snoopy's computer to accept some fuel sources and ignore others, right?"

"Right."

"Next time," I said heavily, "program out the dead stuff."

"Your wish is my command, Widget Woman."

I signed off and clipped the radio back on my web belt. Like Sergeant Cassidy, I was in combat boots and ABUs. ABU, for those of you unacquainted with them, stands for airman battle uniform. Baggy pants and baggy shirt done in pixelated tiger stripes on a heavy fabric that's supposed to reduce the wearer's near-infrared signature. Maybe on the outside. On the inside, I was swimming in sweat.

I'd clipped up my hair and tucked it under my patrol cap, but the thick auburn mane has a mind of its own.

Damp tendrils straggled down my neck, and my face was so slick I had to remove my sunglasses and swipe my cheeks and chin with my sleeve while Snoopy processed his meal.

"We're only a few miles from Pancho's," Sergeant Cassidy commented, hefting the palm-size unit that controlled the robot. "Want me to aim him in that direction?"

"God, yes!"

BAD decision. Reeeally bad.

The dead rat should have tipped me to the possibility that Snoopy might sniff out other, equally unpleasant fuel sources. Which he did, not two minutes after we pulled up at Pancho's.

The crumbling adobe establishment sits on the south side of the only road running through the town of Dry Springs, Texas. Dry Springs is the closest human habitat to my team's isolated test site. We deploy there once a quarter to test weird inventions like Snoopy SNFIR. And while we're at the site, we deploy to Pancho's every chance we get.

Aching for something tall and cool, I swung my leg over the back of the ATV and dismounted, Texas-style. Sergeant Cassidy did the same with considerably more grace and coordination. What can I say? He spends his free time working out. I spend mine watching TV or perusing glamour mags.

Or otherwise occupied with the studly Border Patrol agent I've been seeing for a little more than eight months now. I was thinking that I only had three days left at the test site before I returned to El Paso and the arms of Macho Mitch when I noticed Snoopy banging his snout against a Dumpster off to the side of the dirt parking lot.

"Noel! You'd better corral that thing before he climbs in and we have to dive in after him."

Sergeant Cassidy pushed his patrol cap back on his sweaty forehead and played with the controls. He got Snoopy aimed away from the garbage and zooming in the opposite direction. That's when the omnivorous little critter went for the pickup.

It was dusty and dented, much like the other vehicles driven by the customers who patronize Pancho's. From where I stood, I could see the truck bed contained a jumble of shovels and steel pipes caked with mud. Also the dented beer cooler I mentioned earlier. I assumed a construction crew had stopped at Pancho's to gas up and/or chow down. Snoopy obviously assumed they'd brought him lunch.

He kept trying to mount the pickup's rear wheel. Or hump it. I wasn't sure which as he charged the tire, backed up, and charged again. Several times.

"Oh, for . . . !" Totally exasperated, I flapped a hand at Sergeant Cassidy and hurried over to the truck. "Shut him off before he does something that embarrasses us."

Noel duly killed Snoopy's engine and I bent to pick him up. The whole course of history might have changed if I'd gotten a good grip on his shoebox frame. But I didn't, and Snoop slipped out of my arms. He bounced off the pickup's side rail and thumped down on top of the beer cooler.

I leaned over to retrieve him and had him tucked under my arm again when the door to the bar side of Pancho's establishment slammed back on its hinges. The bear of a man who burst through it came at me in a dead run.

"What the hell you doing?"

"Huh?"

Not the most intelligent response, I admit, but I was so startled by the unexpected attack it was all I could manage at that moment.

"Get away from my pickup!"

I found my voice. Or more correctly, the smart mouth my mother claims I sprang out of the womb with.

"Cool it, pal. I'm not trying to steal your muddy pipes."

"What's that under your arm?"

"Nothing you need to get excited about."

Either he wasn't listening or he didn't believe me. Thrusting his hand under his shirttail, he whipped out a vicious-looking semiautomatic.

"What the fuck have you got under your arm?"

My heart jumped into my throat. My stomach took a simultaneous dive to the toes of my combat boots. Feeling nothing but icy emptiness in between, I held up my free hand and backed away.

"Nothing of yours. I swear. This is . . ."

That's all I got out before Sergeant Cassidy revved his ATV to full power. I hadn't seen him leap back into the saddle, but I certainly saw him tear across the parking lot. Head down, he aimed right for the Bear.

"Noel!" I screamed at the top of my lungs to com-

10

pete with the ATV's roar. "Look out! He's got a gun."

What happened next took five seconds. Ten at the most. But they were the longest seconds of my life!

The Bear spun around. Spotted Noel. Pumped off two shots. The second was still reverberating in my ears when the bar door crashed open again and Pancho let loose with both barrels of the sawed-off shotgun he kept under the counter.

The blast cut the Bear almost in half. He went down in a spray of blood and guts. Noel thumped his ATV over the body before he could kill the engine. My knees folded, and my butt hit the dirt.

For the *next* five or ten seconds, I sat there, stunned, with Snoopy still tucked under one arm. It's not like I'm a stranger to violence. I was just a kid at the time, but I remember my mother laying open my father's scalp with a gin bottle before he took off, never to be seen again. I seriously considered doing the same to my ex, Charlie "Dumbass" Spade, when I caught him with our bimbo neighbor. I refrained, but I have been involved in several nasty incidents since taking over leadership of FST-3. None of which were my fault, I would like to point out, although my boss at DARPA headquarters has become increasingly reluctant to return my phone calls.

This incident had happened so fast, though. I couldn't seem to comprehend it. Still shell-shocked, I struggled to my feet and rushed over to Sergeant Cassidy.

"Noel! Are you okay?"

"Yeah. It's only a flesh wound."

I hadn't even noticed the red staining his upper

thigh! Spinning on my heel, I shouted to Pancho. "He's hit! Get your response kit."

In addition to being the proprietor of the only business establishment in Dry Springs, Pancho also serves as chief of its volunteer fire department. As such, he's fully trained in emergency response procedures. While he rushed back inside the shop, Noel pooh-poohed his wound.

"No need to make a fuss, Lieutenant." He probed the wound with his forefinger. "The mosquitoes in Mogadishu bite deeper than this."

Never having been to Mogadishu, I took his word for that. But I still insisted he climb off the ATV, stretch out in the dirt, and elevate his leg until Pancho reappeared. With Noel horizontal, I approached the Bear. Wasn't much chance he'd survived having his midsection pelletized but I felt compelled to check for a pulse anyway. I didn't find one.

I was back at Noel's side when Pancho returned. His waxed mustache bristling, he knelt in the dirt and peered at the wound with his good eye. A black patch covers the other eye. I'll explain later.

"It's only a flesh wound," he pronounced after cutting through Noel's camos. "Barely creased the skin."

I ignored my sergeant's I-told-you-so look. "Just patch him up."

"While I do that," Pancho said with a sideways glance at the Bear, "you'd better contact Roy Alexander."

I'd interfaced with Sheriff Alexander during one of those nasty incidents I referred to a moment ago. As a result, the El Paso County sheriff evinced only mild surprise when I reported a shooting at Pancho's and said he was on his way.

After that, there was nothing to do but wait. And fill Pancho in on the bizarre sequence of events that had us all squatting in the dirt outside his bar/motel/etc. When I got to the Snoopy part, though, he swiveled on his heel and hitched a disbelieving brow.

"It's a *what*?"

As I said, Dry Springs is the closest town to FST-3's isolated test site. The inhabitants know we test some weird stuff. Like the supposedly safe hyper-optic lens that ignited a major brush fire some months back. So Snoopy held Pancho's fascinated interest while I attempted to explain him.

"It's a self-propelled robot designed to sniff out its own food."

"Now that you mention it," Pancho mused, "it does look like a small coyote."

Pretty apt comparison. Snoopy certainly possessed some of the same characteristics as the scavengers of the desert.

"We're testing it for possible battlefield application."

"So why was it trying to hump the tire on this guy's truck?"

"You saw that, did you?"

He flashed me a quick grin. "Kinda hard to miss, Lootenant."

"I'm not sure what that was all about," I admitted. Lips pursed, I studied the pickup. "For some reason, the robot seemed to think he'd found a fuel source in the bed of the pickup."

Pancho stroked one side of his droopy handlebar mustache. Despite all the expensive wax he applies daily, the tips insist on turning down more often than up. It always reminds me of that cartoon character Yosemite Sam, except Pancho's handle is jet black instead of fire-engine red.

"Any idea what he was after?" he asked, eyeing the dusty pickup.

"No."

My tone implied that it wouldn't be proper to tamper with evidence before Sheriff Alexander arrived. Pancho's tone implied the opposite.

"Maybe we should take a look-see."

I chewed on the inside of my cheek. Thought about the kangaroo rat. Bit down harder.

"Maybe we should."

So I have a lively sense of curiosity? Sue me.

I checked with Noel first to make sure he was comfortable. I also checked the pad covering his wound. No fresh, bright blood stained the gauze. Confident my sergeant would survive to continue his sessions with his shrink, I pushed to my feet and joined Pancho.

He's an inch or two shorter than I am. Five-six or -seven to my five-seven. But he's tough and wiry and very reassuring to have at your side when approaching a pickup with suspicious contents.

The dented red beer cooler drew my immediate attention. Looking back, I'm not sure what I expected to find when I lifted the lid. A skinned and butchered deer maybe. Or the feathered carcass of one of the endangered Northern Aplomado falcons so prized by poachers on both sides of the border. Certainly not three disembodied heads turning a moldy green!

When the aroma that shot out of the cooler hit me, I slammed the lid down and promptly contaminated the crime scene by throwing up. Pancho jumped back just in time to keep from getting his boots similarly contaminated.

CHAPTER TWO

BY the time Sheriff Alexander arrived, Sergeant Cassidy was on his feet and word of the shooting had spread through Dry Springs.

Thirty-seven inquisitive souls had gathered in the dirt parking lot. They constituted the town's entire population, less two kids bussed to school some twenty miles away and Eloisa Rivera, currently visiting her daughter in San Diego. The crowd batted absently at flies and speculated on the identity of the Bear, now covered with an oil-stained canvas, as well as the other three deceased.

I knew most of the folks in the crowd. My team and I had shared beers with the regulars who hung out at the bar and had met the others during stops at the convenience store side of Pancho's establishment. They pretty much took the Bear's corpse in stride. Violence has become a fact of life this close to the U.S.-Mexico border. The severed heads fascinated them, though.

Speculation ran rife about who the deceased were and how they'd ended up in the beer cooler. I caught snatches of conversation that touched on everything from the drug wars raging just south of us to a *Silence of the Lambs*–type cannibal with gruesome appetites. I also caught more than one glance aimed at Snoopy. I'd kept mum about *his* taste in snacks but rumors were already circulating. The arrival of a black-and-white spared me a public explanation.

Sheriff Alexander emerged from the cruiser and settled his straw Stetson low on his brow. Like so many in this part of the country, his face is all weathered skin and white squint lines. After greeting Pancho, he turned to me and tipped two fingers to his hat brim.

"Hello, Samantha. What's with you and corpses?"

He was referring to the decomposing bodies I'd stumbled across while testing another invention last year. Or maybe the rogue FBI agent who ran Mitch and me into an arroyo and got dead as a result. Or the ex-Army sergeant who'd tried to gun down his lover until I threw off his aim.

"I don't know," I replied with some feeling, "but I've bagged my limit for the foreseeable future."

Nodding, the sheriff approached the canvas and hunkered down on his heels. He lifted the tarp and studied the Bear for several moments before swiveling around to examine the semiautomatic lying in the dirt a few feet away. The contents of the cooler warranted a longer look before the sheriff turned to the crowd.

"Anyone recognize these people?"

Head shakes all around.

"Anyone besides the lieutenant, her sergeant, and Pancho here see what happened?"

More head shakes.

"All right, then. Y'all go get out of the sun and let me talk to these three."

A few of the onlookers went home. Most of them crowded into the bar, determined not to miss out on the excitement. Pancho, Noel, and I remained in place.

As you might expect, Snoopy's role in the sequence of events elicited a disbelieving grunt from the sheriff. He surveyed the SNFIR, its ears drooping in the afternoon heat, and pushed his Stetson to the back of his head.

"You and your team test some weird stuff, Lieutenant."

"Tell me about it."

He ruminated for a moment, sorting through our statements and his own impressions of the crime scene. "You say the vic fired first?"

"He did," I confirmed. "Two shots. One hit Sergeant Cassidy before Pancho, er, took him out."

"I'll need to bag that shotgun as evidence, Panch."

"No problem."

No problem, we all knew, because he keeps a backup. Or three. Or five. This is West Texas, remember.

"Not much more we can do here until the coroner arrives," Alexander announced. "I'll stay with the bodies. Y'all might as well go inside and cool off."

My radio squawked on my way across the parking lot. I unhooked it from my belt with some reluctance. I had a pretty good idea how the rest of my team would react to this unexpected turn of events. I should. I've plunged them into several similarly bizarre situations in the months we've been together.

"Lieutenant Spade," I acknowledged.

"We aren't receiving signals from SNFIR. What's going on?"

The voice on the other end belonged to Dr. Brian "Rocky" Balboa, our nervous little twitch of a test engineer. Rock's a good guy. Mostly. But he can be a major pain in the bohunkus when it comes to following prescribed test protocols.

"We've run into, uh, a glitch."

"Glitch?"

Amazing how a single echo can convey so many nuances. I heard instant wariness, incipient dread, and more than a touch of resignation.

"Noel and I are at Pancho's," I explained. "There's been a shooting and . . ."

"A shooting! Are you okay?"

"I am, but Noel was wounded."

"They're at Pancho's," I heard Rocky shout to the rest of my team, his voice spiraling up two full octaves. "Noel's been shot."

Wincing at the shrill screech, I tried to assure him Sergeant Cassidy was up and walking and pooh-poohing his mosquito bite. Didn't work. Rock tends to get a tad agitated. When *really* excited or nervous, he also tends to expel gas. Big, noxious bloopers that can clear a room in ten seconds flat. I gave silent but very fervent thanks we were communicating via radio.

"We're on our way," he informed me in a rush.

"Wait, Rock. You don't need to . . ."

Too late. He'd slammed the radio down. I heard the sounds of a small stampede and resigned myself to the imminent arrival of the rest of my team.

THEY weren't long in coming.

Our test site is just over ten miles from Dry Springs. Noel and I had been scuttling through the backcountry for hours on our ATVs, chasing Snoopy over hill and dale. Our fellow team members jumped into one of the vans we use to transport supplies and equipment and hit the tarmac. They arrived at Pancho's mere moments after the county coroner's team, which had drawn all interested spectators outside again.

I have to confess I was glad to see my troops. Despite our individual idiosyncrasies—and we have many!— the five members of FST-3 have more or less bonded. More, when our tests and evaluations are going well. Less, on those infrequent occasions I attempt to exert my authority as team leader.

That's the thing about being a second lieutenant. People have a hard time taking you seriously. Especially braniac civilians like Dennis O'Reilly, Rocky Balboa, and Penelope England. With his frizzy orange hair and black-framed nerdo glasses, you would think O'Reilly would be the one with a credibility gap. Or Rocky with his owl-eyed stare and thin, twitchy shoulders.

No one ever questions Pen's credibility, however. And not just because of her two PhDs and ability to deliver long, detailed lectures on almost any subject. Dr. Penelope England is Earth Mother incarnate. Calm and placid and sturdy in her Birkenstocks and multilayers of natural linen. True, she has a tendency to skewer her lopsided, salt-and-pepper bun with whatever implement is handy. We once spent hours searching for a soil moisture probe before we thought to check her hair. Also true, she has a neighing laugh that makes everyone within hearing distance wish fervently they weren't.

But Pen wasn't laughing when she piled out of the van with Dennis and Rocky. Her thick-soled sandals sent up little puffs of dirt as she and the others rushed across the parking lot.

Pancho noted their arrival and ambled over to join us.

Editorial aside here. I've recently become aware there might be something going on between Pen and Pancho and have yet to recover from the shock. Nor have I heard anything definitive from my sexy Border Patrol agent, who promised to check out rumors Pancho left behind at least one wife, possibly more, when he decamped from Mexico an unknown number of years ago.

Supposedly, that's how Pancho lost his eye. Or one version of the story, anyway. Some swear his angry wife gouged it out after catching him with another woman. I certainly wouldn't blame her if she had. I'd come pretty darn close to mayhem myself after catching Charlie "Bonehead" Spade in the same nauseating circumstances.

But others contend Pancho got poked in the eye during a riot after a soccer match. Whatever the cause, there's no getting around the fact that the eye *not* covered by a black patch lit up when it spotted Pen. I noticed the gleam, but none of the other team members did. They had totally focused on the blood staining Sergeant Cassidy's ABU pants.

The rusty splotches pursed Pen's lips. Rocky swiped a nervous palm across his thinning sandy hair. O'Reilly turned pale and hooked a finger in the neck of his black T-shirt stamped with the image of his hero, world chess champion and weirdo supreme Bobby Fischer.

After assuring themselves that Noel wasn't in immediate need of a transfusion or—this from Pen—a cup of specially infused herbal tea, they peppered us with questions.

"What happened?"

"Who's under that canvas tarp?"

"Is he the one who shot Noel?"

Before I could answer, Dennis O'Reilly angled his head and peered through his inch-thick lenses. "What's the coroner removing from that beer cooler? Is that . . . ?" His eyes bugged out. "Good God, is that a *head*?"

"It is," I responded, sincerely hoping I wouldn't contaminate the crime scene again. "One of three inside that cooler."

Dennis, Rocky, and Pen gaped at me, then Pancho, then me again. Pen was the first to recover.

"Really, Samantha." She patted my shoulder sympathetically. "You certainly have a propensity for landing in the most unusual situations."

Unusual was her way of describing them. I'd go with freaky.

We watched the proceedings until the heat got to us, then I secured Snoopy in the van and we all trooped

inside the bar. If you ever want to assault every one of
your senses at the same time, just plunge from the bright
light of a May afternoon into the perpetual gloom of
Pancho's bar. All kinds of scents flavor the air. Stale
cigarette smoke predominates, although you can always
catch a whiff of the green chili stew Pancho brews daily.
The music alternates between salsa and country. Both
sound equally tinny coming through ancient speakers
strung with drooping wires. Flyspecked neon abounds,
but it's the wall art that drops most newcomers' jaws.

Centerfolds from decades' worth of *Sports Illustrated*
Swimsuit Editions cover every vertical surface. Most of
the ceiling, too. The regulars are used to the decor. We
don't even notice all those near-naked thighs and chests.
What I *did* notice, however, was the sheepish grin on
Pancho's face when he reached under the stained oak
counter and produced a china teapot. It had roses on it, I
saw with disbelief. Pink ones.

"I spotted this at an antique shop over to San An-
gelo," he informed Pen as she settled on a bar stool.
"It's got a strainer thing inside it."

Those of us regularly subjected to Dr. Penelope
England's herbal concoctions could have told him the
piece he extracted and held up for her inspection is
called an infuser. Pen merely smiled her approval.

"It's lovely, Pancho. Thank you for thinking of me.
Do you still have any of the lemongrass and sumac
blend I brought you?"

"Sure do. Want me to brew you a pot?"

"Yes, please."

While he fussed with tea leaves and hot water,

Rocky, Dennis, Noel, and I did a collective gape. We get beer in bottles or tequila shooters in cloudy shot glasses. Pen gets pink roses.

Suspicion confirmed. There's definitely something going on between those two. I'm not sure I really want to know what, though.

I picked up my beer with an odd, disconnected sense. Here I sat, surrounded by swimsuit models and tables topped with chipped Formica while Pancho brewed tea in an antique china pot and the county coroner bagged a corpse and three severed heads outside. Things don't get much stranger than that.

OR so I thought. The arrival of a round-faced, profusely perspiring reporter less than five minutes later gave the weird screw another twist. He stopped dead just inside the door, as did most first-timers. His mouth went slack, and you could almost hear his vertebrae pop as he craned his neck to take in the decor. While he surveyed the scenery, we surveyed him.

He couldn't have been more than twenty-two or -three. Below the waist, he wore sensible boots and jeans. Above, a not-so-sensible navy blazer and pale yellow shirt with a button-down collar. The patch on the blazer's pocket identified him as a member of Channel Nine News. The sweat dripping from his chin told me he'd already surveyed the scene in the parking lot.

Tearing his gaze from the wall art, he searched the gloom and made tracks for the bar. "Excuse me. Are you Lieutenant Spade?"

I glanced down at the name tape stitched above my uniform pocket. Glanced back at Junior Reporter. Arched a brow.

"Maybe."

I'd learned the hard way to watch every word around the media. Even my most innocent statements have a way of coming back to bite me in the butt. That could be doubly true in this instance, given that I was in uniform and had my hand wrapped around a dew-streaked beer.

"I'm DeWayne Wilson, Channel Nine News."

He thrust out a hand. I'm wary but not totally without couth. I let him encase my bottle-dampened palm with his sweaty one. The niceties over with, we both surreptitiously swiped our hands on our pants legs.

"I usually work high school sports," he confided with the eagerness of a puppy. "I just finished covering a track-and-field meet in Fort Davis and was on my way back to El Paso when the boss heard about the shooting on the police scanner. He sent me here."

"Lucky you."

My sarcasm zinged right over his head.

"I know!" he exclaimed. "This is my first shooting. It could be my big break."

Uh-oh. Young, eager, and hot to get into hard news. This was Not Good.

"Sheriff Alexander told me you discovered the heads, Lieutenant. My cameraman's out in the parking lot. Would you come outside so I could interview you?"

"Sorry. Military personnel aren't allowed to comment on their involvement in ongoing investigations."

That was stretching the truth a bit. We're allowed to comment—if we want to put our careers on the line. My career is iffy at best, but there was no way in hell I wanted to hear my role in this bizarre incident dissected on the evening news. Or, more important, Snoopy's role. Somehow I suspected the viewing public wasn't ready for a rat-devouring robot.

"You'll have to go through the Public Affairs office at Fort Bliss," I told the crestfallen DeWayne.

He turned to Sergeant Cassidy. "I guess that includes you, too."

Given Noel's run-in with an undercover vice cop and ongoing sessions with his shrink, I wasn't surprised when he evinced even less eagerness to appear in front of a TV camera than I had.

"Yeah, it does."

"What about you?" the now-desperate reporter asked Pancho. "The sheriff wouldn't confirm who shot the pickup driver, but several of the people I talked to said you pulled the trigger. Will you comment for the record?"

Pancho twisted up one corner of his mustache and gave the kid a blank look. *"No hablo Inglés."*

Junior Reporter's face fell. "I could, um, find a translator."

The suggestion met with another blank look.

I could tell DeWayne's dreams of making it out of high school track-and-field were disintegrating before his eyes. I felt sorry for him, but not sorry enough to put myself or Snoop Dog in front of a camera.

Dejected, he mumbled an insincere thank-you and

left. Pen went back to her tea, the rest of us to our beer, tequila, and/or soft drinks.

I knew it wasn't over. This head business was too sensational for the media to pass up. Still, I was in no way, shape, or form prepared for the firestorm that proceeded to engulf me.

CHAPTER THREE

THE first sinister rumblings of the storm hit not long after my team and I returned to our test site.

Don't let the grandiose designation fool you. The site consists of five Containerized Housing Units—aka CHUs—plunked down on a remote corner of the Fort Bliss missile range. There they sat when we drove up a little past seven p.m., five aluminum-sided boxcars surrounded by shadowy cacti and spiny creosote. Our home away from home.

Two of the CHUs serve as sleeping quarters—one for the guys, one for Pen and me. Two more are linked together to form our test lab and administrative center. The fifth is our D-FAC. Officially the acronym stands for dining facility. Unofficially it . . . Well, I'd better not go there.

The D-FAC contains a kitchen of sorts, a handkerchief-sized dining table, a flat-screen TV hooked up to a satellite dish, a DVD player, various board games, wireless routers for our laptops, and taking up twice its fair share of floor space, Sergeant Cassidy's Universal Gym.

Noel's gunshot wound produced one unexpected benefit. Slight though it was, the injury kept him from clanking away on his weights all evening long. Thus we were able to both watch and hear the ten p.m. news coverage of the shooting.

As I'd anticipated, the local networks glommed on to the heads. But Channel Nine had scored a coup by diverting DeWayne Wilson out to Dry Springs. His was the only report with actual on-scene footage, such as it was.

Junior Reporter got shots of the pickup being towed away and the coroner's wagon as it drove off. He also had his cameraman pan the facade of Pancho's. The place looked considerably more decrepit on screen than it did when you drove up, hot and dusty and thirsting for something cold.

"Although all persons involved in the shooting declined to be interviewed on-camera," DeWayne intoned solemnly, "this reporter can confirm one of them is Air Force Lieutenant Samantha Spade. Viewers might remember her from another shooting incident last year."

I grimaced as my picture filled the screen. It was a stock photo dredged from the news coverage of the incident DeWayne cited. To my disgust, I looked wild-eyed and more like a shooter than a shootee.

"Forensic specialists hope dental impressions and facial recognition software will identify the severed heads. In the meantime, the FBI's regional office has made a tentative identification of the alleged shooter."

"That didn't take long," Dennis commented.

My face disappeared and the camera cut to the El Paso Regional FBI Office. An all-too-familiar figure strode toward a bank of mikes.

"Hey." Dennis adjusted his Coke-bottle lenses for a closer look and shot me a quick glance. "Isn't that your pal?"

My stomach did a quick roll as Special Agent Paul Donati looked into the cameras. Pals we weren't. Donati and I had locked horns on previous occasions when I mucked around in an official investigation. His words, not mine. I was completely innocent this time, but his eyes seemed to spear right through me as he issued a brief statement.

"I can confirm that the FBI has made a tentative ID. We're withholding that ID, however, pending notification of the next of kin."

Reporters peppered him with questions, but he had nothing more to add. I breathed a sigh of relief. Too soon, it turned out.

"In what has to be one of the most bizarre aspects of an already bizarre incident," Junior Reporter gushed when his cameraman cut back to him, "it appears the, um, body parts may have been nosed out by a robot."

"Oh, no!"

My stomach took another plunge. So much for keeping Snoopy's role in this incident away from the viewing public.

Apparently DeWayne had pumped various residents

of Dry Springs for detail. He'd also conducted an Internet search and nosed out Farmer Farnsworth's website. I cringed as wild rumor gave way to even wilder speculation. And I knew I was in trouble when Junior Reporter described Snoop as a flesh-eating robot.

"The implications are staggering," he intoned, wide-eyed. "Just think of it. A vehicle that could feed on battlefield corpses and go forever."

Groaning, I dropped my head to the table and covered it with both arms. I guessed it was only a matter of hours, if not minutes, before my cell phone started pinging.

I was right.

The first call came from my studly Border Patrol agent. I've assigned him a special ringtone. It's the theme from the Clint Eastwood spaghetti Western *Hang 'Em High*, which pretty well sums up what Mitch does for a living. His image popped into my head with the first few notes. Tall, rangy, with white squint lines at the corners of his hazel eyes. Those little lines crinkle when he grins, but I could tell from his response to my chirpy hello that he wasn't smiling at the moment.

"Jesus, Samantha! What have you gotten mixed up in now?"

That seemed pretty unfair, seeing as Jeff Mitchell had figured prominently in my previous two encounters with persons of the dead variety. When I said so, however, he brushed my tart observation aside.

"This has all the earmarks of a murder for hire. Don't get any more involved than you already are. Let Paul Donati handle it."

"I intend to."

"I heard Sergeant Cassidy took a bullet. How's he doing?"

I glanced at Noel. Although his leg wound kept him out of the iron cage, he'd stripped down to his T-shirt, planted an elbow on the table, and was doing curls with a twenty-pound dumbbell while watching the news coverage.

"Mitch wants to know how you're doing."

Biceps bulging, he nodded. "Tell him I'm fine."

"He's fine."

"Good. So when are you coming home?"

"We should wrap things up Friday afternoon."

"I've got patrol Friday night." Mitch's gruff tone softened. "How about I swing by your place after debrief Saturday morning?"

"Sounds good," I replied as little shivers of anticipation danced down my spine.

"I'll see you then."

I spent a happy five minutes or so envisioning all kinds of matutinal delights. Did I mention that Mitch is really well toned?

When my cell phone jangled again, one glance at caller ID wiped every salacious thought from my mind. Swallowing, I hit answer.

"Hi, Paul." As in Special Agent Donati. "I just saw you on Channel Six. Have you really made a tentative ID?"

"The alleged shooter is Victor Duarte. We've withheld his identity . . ."

"Pending next of kin," I supplied helpfully.

"The bastard has no next of kin. None that we've turned up, anyway. We held back his ID to give us time to try to track his movements until he showed up in Dry Springs."

"Have you?"

"Not yet." He paused a moment. "This guy's a real badass, Samantha. A contract killer."

"That's what Mitch guessed."

"Mitch got it right." Another pause, followed by a terse question. "Have you checked the FBI's Most Wanted website lately?"

"I didn't know you *had* a Most Wanted website."

"We do. You might want to take a look at it."

"Because . . . ?"

"Because Duarte is number two on our list. The FBI is offering a hundred-thousand-dollar reward for information leading to his capture and/or arrest."

"What!"

My mind spun like the wheels of the slot machines at my prior place of employment

"Capture?" I squeaked out, seeking clarification. "Does that mean, um, dead or alive?"

"Dead or alive."

Dollar signs flashed in front of my eyes. Mesmerized, I was envisioning all the ways I could stimulate the economy, when reality set in.

"You do know Pancho was the one who took him down, don't you?"

"Pancho claims he wouldn't have fired if you and Sergeant Cassidy hadn't flushed the bastard out. Far as

I know, the reward is yours to split however you three work it out."

The dollar signs lit up again. In avocado-toned neon this time!

Let me insert a small caveat here. I don't consider myself particularly materialistic. I'm very content in my small El Paso apartment. I drive a relatively new Sebring convertible. It used to be bright and shiny and undented until I deliberately rammed the vehicle of a bad guy trying to make a getaway a few months back. That, sadly, eliminated its new-car aura, but it's been repaired and can still go from zero to sixty in mere seconds. And since I spend most of my waking hours in uniform, I don't need a closet full of expensive finery.

Although . . .

If I had a big wad of dollars to blow, I might just splurge on several pairs of Stuart Weitzmans or Kate Spades. After clumping around in combat boots all day, I usually go the flip flop route. Some really expensive, really girly footwear would make for a nice change.

I might also lipo-suck away the teeny-weeny dimples I recently discovered on my thighs. How and when they got there is a total mystery. Just a little over eighteen months ago I was collecting major tips while prancing around in a short skirt and ruffled panties that showed off firm, un-dimpled thighs. But I hit the big three-oh some months ago. Now I avoid looking at my lower extremities in a mirror whenever possible.

Once restored to my former sleekness, I mused, I might just whisk Mitch off for a week or two in one of those luxurious Tahitian over-the-water bungalows I saw recently on the Travel Channel. Best I recall, they went for around eighteen hundred a night, plus change.

Lets see. Ten or twelve nights at eighteen hundred bucks. That came to . . .

Special Agent Donati broke into my happy calculations. "You need to be careful, Samantha. Duarte was a real slime. Whoever hired him to make these hits falls into the same category."

That was one way to bring me back to earth. Pancho laid another on me when I called him right after Donati and I disconnected.

"Did you catch the news?"

"No."

A rattle of glass punctuated his reply. Empty beer bottles, I guessed. Or Pen's rose-covered teapot. The mental image that conjured up almost made me forget why I'd called.

"I suppose we were the lead story," Pancho commented, pulling me back to the present.

"And then some! The FBI IDed the shooter. His name is Victor Duarte."

There was a small silence. It didn't occur to me until that moment I might have gotten involved in something more than a chance encounter with a gun-wielding stranger. Pancho's past is nothing if not murky. My heart skipped several beats and all kinds of unwelcome thoughts cartwheeled through my mind until he responded.

"Never heard of the guy."

I let out a slow breath. I would never deflate Pancho's

swaggering machivity by telling him so, but he's become something of father figure to me. Maybe it's a result of his years of tending bar. Or the sympathetic gleam in his good eye when I start to complain about life in general and the military in particular. Or it could be that he's more involved in my life than my real father was. Not that Dad had much time to get involved before Mom chased him off with a gin bottle. Whatever the reason, I didn't want to believe Pancho was mixed up in anything shadier than the high-stakes poker game that took place in the bar's back room every Saturday night.

"According to Special Agent Donati," I told him, "Duarte is a hired killer."

"Must be why he was toting those heads around with him," Pancho mused with apparent unconcern. "Proof he'd completed the job."

"Must be. There's more."

Cash registers started ka-chinging in my head again and an excited note crept into my voice.

"Donati said the FBI was offering a hundred-thousand-dollar reward for information leading to Duarte's capture and arrest."

"*How* much?"

"A hundred thousand. You and Noel and I may be eligible to claim it."

The silence was longer this time. Way longer.

"I'll have to think about that," Pancho said at last.

I hung up, wondering what there was to think about.

Only gradually did it dawn on Noel and me and the rest of FST-3 that claiming the reward might create the kind of nightmare that can only occur in bureaucratic circles. In short order, Noel and I progressed from making wish lists to speculating on whether we could accept a reward since we were in uniform, on duty, and conducting official business when Duarte lined us up in his sights.

"Maybe I can find something online."

I pulled up the FBI website and skimmed down a long, scary list of "most wanteds." I couldn't find anything on how to collect on them, though, so I clicked on a tab for a program called Rewards for Justice. That took me to a different site. This one listed international terrorists and the amounts offered for information leading to their capture and arrest. The twenty-five-million-dollar bounty for Osama bin Laden made our hundred thousand seem like loose change!

I paged through the rest of the site and discovered it was funded by private donations. And there, in bold print, was a prohibition against payments to anyone who worked for the U.S. government in any capacity.

I clicked back to the FBI website, but couldn't find a similar prohibition. That gave us a momentary boost—until Rocky reminded us of who we worked for.

DARPA has this strict code of ethics. It addresses in excruciating detail what employees can and can't accept from companies or agencies seeking to do business with us. Demonstrations of new technologies are a yes. Free donuts and coffee during these demos are a no.

Who knew where a hundred grand in reward money fell on the list? I certainly didn't. I went to bed later that evening wondering about it, though.

* * *

WHEN my phone pinged early the next morning, I checked caller ID and toyed briefly with the wild notion of asking my boss about the reward. That lasted only until I flipped up the phone, hit the video display, and saw the haunted expression on his face.

Poor Dr. Jessup. I've put him through the wringer several times in our professional association. I never *intend* to make him reach for the aspirin and Pepto-Bismol. And it's not that I don't like the man. I do! I also admire him tremendously. I mean, how many Harvard heavies with a mind-boggling string of degrees would take a zillion percent pay cut to work for the U.S. government?

Unfortunately for Dr. J, he arrived at DARPA the same week I did. We both suspect that's how he got stuck supervising a lowly lieutenant minus even a master's degree. He didn't know enough to duck and run.

He's had to duck a number of times since. Judging by the look on his face, this was evidently one of those times.

"Samantha," he got out in a choked voice. "Tell me it's not true."

What wasn't true? The shooting? The disembodied heads? Sergeant Cassidy's gunshot wound? Since I couldn't reassure him on any of the above points, I resorted to chewing on the inside of my cheek.

"Please," he pleaded. "Please confirm you're not testing a flesh-eating robot."

"Well . . ."

"I knew it!" He let out a moan. "When they brought up Article Twenty of the Geneva Convention, I knew we were in trouble!"

I'd heard of the Geneva Convention, of course. Every military recruit is briefed on its general provisions and the Code of Ethics that evolved from it. Among other things, the code forbids U.S. military personnel from revealing more than their name, rank, and serial number if captured by the enemy. Unless—and this is a big caveat here!—we're tortured beyond our ability to resist.

"Article Twenty?" I echoed in a hollow voice as visions of rubber hoses and electrified nipple clamps flitted through my head.

"The war crimes section." Dr. J's expression turned anguished above his red and white polka-dot bow tie. "Among other things, it prohibits desecration of the dead. Which, if the wild stories emanating from Texas are to be believed, your robot does."

CHAPTER FOUR

NEEDLESS to say, the moment I got off the phone with Dr. J I powered up my laptop and Googled the Geneva Convention. I was surprised to discover there are actually four of them, all setting standards of international law for the humanitarian treatment of victims of war.

The first treaty came about after the 1862 publication of a book titled *Memoir of Solferino*. Based on his own horrific experiences in battle, the author pushed for a permanent relief agency to aid war victims and a government treaty recognizing the neutrality of such an agency. That led to the founding of the International Red Cross and the original Geneva Convention. These momentous accomplishments won the author the co-honor of the first Nobel Peace Prize in 1901.

Subsequent treaties addressed members of the armed

forces at sea, the protection of prisoners of war, and—after the 1949 Nuremberg Trials—crimes committed against civilians during wartime.

This was all extremely heavy reading for a second lieutenant. Particularly one whose closest exposure to a combat zone was her frequent shopping excursions across the Rio Grande. Swallowing hard, I spent several hours on the section dealing with collective punishments and reprisals for desecration of the dead.

I was still hard at it when the crap hit the fan.

I'm talking a huge mountain of it, fanned by the really big blower otherwise known as the wire services. Turns out both AP and Reuters picked up Junior Reporter's story about a flesh-eating robot. Once that bombshell went out over the wires, news agencies and Internet addicts across the country jumped on it. The headlines and blog entries went from disbelieving to downright ghoulish.

The calls came fast and furious after that. I heard from reporters and magazine editors and bloggers and self-proclaimed vampires and one *very* scary necrophiliac. Him I turned over to Paul Donati. The rest I referred to the Public Affairs office at DARPA Headquarters as ordered.

With so much controversy swirling, DARPA felt compelled to issue a statement. In it they confirmed that the agency had funded neither the research for nor the development of SNFIR. Nor did it condone in any way a device that consumed human remains.

This avalanche of negative PR prompted a fierce rebuttal from Snoopy's extremely agitated inventor. Farnsworth held a hastily convened news conference outside his barn/workshop in Idaho. Acres of brown potato fields formed the backdrop. An affiliate of Channel Nine covered the story, which they aired on the early evening newscast.

Once again all five members of FST-3 gathered in the D-FAC to watch. The air conditioner blasted us with chilled air while Farmer Farnsworth blasted us with charges ranging from carelessness to total incompetence.

"I included precise operating instructions with SNFIR," he said indignantly. "Also a detailed appendix listing every potential fuel source."

I ignored Dennis O'Reilly's pointed look.

"All those people had to do was program SNFIR to identify and consume acceptable fuel sources while ignoring others," the inventor continued with a disgusted shake of his head. "Any third grader could do it."

Lips pooched, I glanced at the members of my team. One double PhD with an IQ somewhere out there in the stratosphere. Another PhD in the person of Rocky, our test engineer. A software genius with an ability to string together lines of code completely incomprehensible to ordinary mortals. A staff sergeant who's racked up umpteen years of military service. The closest thing to a third grader in the group was me.

"If high-paid government scientists can't figure out how to operate a simple device like SNFIR," Farnsworth huffed, "this country's in trouble."

Ha! Showed what farmers knew about government

employee pay scales. Thoroughly pissed on behalf of my team, I stalked over to my laptop.

"What are you doing?" Pen asked.

"Emailing a certain potato farmer to let him know I don't appreciate his remarks."

"Better not," she advised, poking absently at her scalp with a chewed-on plastic straw. "You'll only add fuel to the fire."

I didn't care. I don't mind criticism. Probably because I'm on the receiving end of so much of it. But I was darned if I'd let Farnsworth bad-mouth my team. We might be mostly rejects from polite society, but we were professional rejects, dammit.

The email proved to be a little tricky to compose as Sheriff Alexander had asked us to retain possession of Snoop pending completion of his investigation. I was trying to balance my righteous indignation with an explanation of why we couldn't return Farmer Farnsworth's baby when the scene switched back to the Channel Nine newsroom. There was DeWayne in his navy blazer, riding his story for all it was worth.

"In a late-breaking development, the FBI has released the identities of all four victims in this bizarre case. The individual who died in the shooting is Victor Duarte, a career criminal and alleged contract killer suspected in at least a dozen murders for hire."

The Bear's mug shot flashed up on screen. Knowing what I now did about him, I have to admit I wasn't sorry Pancho had taken dead aim on his midsection.

"The mutilated corpses have also been tentatively identified," Junior Reporter informed us. "All three are

Mexican nationals suspected of conducting a multimillion-dollar drug operation in Wisconsin."

I gaped at the screen in disbelief. Those of us living close to the border had grown used to hearing about the viciously warring cartels and major drug busts so close to us. But Wisconsin? Naive soul that I am, it shocked the heck out of me to know the sickness we saw so much of in the border regions had spread that far north.

"The details on the ring are still emerging," DeWayne related solemnly. "We'll update you as we get more information. In the meantime, we've learned the FBI had offered a substantial reward for information leading to Duarte's capture or arrest."

At that point, he jettisoned the objectivity he was trying so hard to project and gushed into the mike.

"Talk about winning the lottery! Someone's gonna collect big bucks on this one."

"Way to go, DeWayne." Disgusted, I shook my head. "Splash it all over TV land, why don't you?"

I still wasn't sure whether Noel or I could claim any portion of the reward. With all the calls and controversy, I hadn't had the time—or the nerve—to check with headquarters about that. This stuff about war crimes and desecration of the dead weighed a lot more heavily on my mind than a closet full of new shoes.

I stuck to my guns over the next few days and refused all requests for information or interviews, referring inquisitors instead to DARPA's Public Affairs office.

Unfortunately, I wasn't as successful at fending off

my family. One of my cousins had read about the triple decapitation/shooting/reward on an ex-con's blog and spread the word to the rest of the clan. My brother, Don, wasted no time in calling.

"I know this really good lawyer," he advised.

Don is four years older than I am and, along with my mom, has been in AA for more than a decade. After a number of abrupt career transitions, he's now a financial advisor in Ventura, California. And we wonder how the economy ended up in the toilet!

"I don't need a lawyer, Don."

"Yeah, ya do, Sammy. This lawyer is good. Remember the twenty grand in back taxes the IRS tried to stick me with a couple years back? He got 'em to accept less than five thousand."

I chose not to remind him that taxes paid for roads and parks and the schools his five kids were yawning their way through.

"Give Nowatny a call," he urged. "He'll get you every penny of that reward."

"Minus his fee, of course."

"Of course. Bastard hit me up for forty percent of the amount IRS knocked off."

"And what do you get out of this deal, Don?"

"You're not going to begrudge me a small referral fee, are you? That's how things work in the real world. Got a pencil? I'll give you Nowatny's number."

The only pencil in sight was the one protruding from Pen's lopsided bun. I didn't reach for it, as I had no intention of contacting Lawyer Nowatny. I pretended otherwise, though, to get my bother off my back. He rattled off the number and issued a final warning.

"Better call him or you'll have every leech and charity case in the family coming at you with their hands out."

Riiiight.

DESPITE the hassles and outside interruptions, my team and I managed to complete the rest of our evaluations by Friday noon as scheduled. None of the remaining items on our list demonstrated potential for military application in a desert environment. I did see real utility, though, in a neat little iPhone-type application that zeroed in on the location of the nearest public restroom.

Of all the items we evaluated, Snoopy had the greatest possibilities. I could envision a hundred uses for him. Assuming we could get him to function within guidelines of the Geneva Convention and not creep everyone out.

With that goal in mind, I got over my snit at Farmer Farnsworth and finally sent him a much-edited email. In it I requested additional time to complete our evaluations. This time, I promised, we would carefully screen Snoopy's menu and take extreme measures to avoid negative publicity. I didn't detail those measures, mostly because I hadn't formulated them yet, but I did win an extension from the disgruntled potato planter.

Then I had to convince a very skeptical Dr. J to let us

give Snoop another shot. That took considerably more effort. Like me, he'd spent a fair number of hours perusing the Geneva Convention. We'd both received a thorough and very nerve-wracking education. But when my team packed up Friday afternoon, Snoopy went with us instead of getting shipped home.

Normally we convoy back to El Paso. Sergeant Cassidy drives his pickup loaded with our personal gear, Dennis the van crammed with our portable equipment. Rocky usually rides with Dennis. Pen cruises home with me.

I much prefer her company to the others on the drive to and from El Paso. She doesn't twitch and start to sweat like Rocky does every time I skim a curve. Nor does she keep a running tally of how much I've forked over for speeding tickets, like Dennis. It's a trade-off, though. Instead of nervous or sarcastic comments, I get lengthy monologues on various topics dear to Pen's heart.

This time, however, she'd driven her own vehicle out to the site. We'd all wondered about that, as she's into her second term as president of the El Paso chapter of Citizens United for a Greener Biosphere and is always on our case about carpooling to reduce our carbon footprint. After that business with the antique teapot, though, I wasn't surprised when we made our obligatory farewell stop at Pancho's and Pen decided to linger awhile.

"You sure?" I asked while Pancho tried to look as innocent as a guy with a black eye patch and waxed handlebar mustache can.

"I'm sure."

"Okay. Well. Um. Drive carefully," I finished lamely.

Pen merely smiled, but everyone else within earshot let loose with a chorus of hoots and catcalls at hearing that advice coming from me. I ignored them, made a dignified exit, and slid behind the wheel of my Sebring convertible.

My insurance company had balked at writing the convertible off as a total loss after I'd used it as a battering ram. They'd replaced the engine, though, and hammered out the dents. I missed its delicious new-car smell but couldn't complain too much as I'd put the top down before we left our site and the predominant scent right now was baked leather. I wiggled my fanny from side to side until the bucket seat cooled enough to settle both cheeks.

Eager to hit the road, I tossed my patrol cap on the passenger seat and slipped on my wraparound sunglasses. I wanted to remove the clip anchoring my hair and let it blow in the wind. Unfortunately, allowing so much as a stray strand to touch your uniform collar is one of the many mysterious military no-no's. This one makes absolutely no sense to me. I suspect it was promulgated by the same jerk who decided female cadets at the service academies should wear pants in marching formation instead of skirts. Heaven forbid we should show some leg and look like women instead of mutant males.

With that bit of internal editorializing out of my system, I keyed the ignition and peeled out of the parking lot. The guys followed at a more sedate speed.

I might as well have unclipped my hair. The wind tugged most of it loose anyway during the drive to El

Paso. It's just a little over eighty miles as the crow flies. We wingless humanoids have to navigate a series of two-lane county roads north, then west, then north again until we finally reach I-10.

This circuitous route takes us through several topological zones. As Pen has reminded my team on numerous occasions, the Chihuahuan Desert is the largest desert in North America. It stretches from just south of Albuquerque through Arizona and Texas all the way down to Mexico City. I must admit I never paid much attention to such matters as topographical zones pre-Pen. I've become a reluctant expert, though, after all her monologues.

Go ahead. Ask me about the growth patterns of the Bigtooth maples that flame with fall color in high mountain canyons. Or a plant group entirely composed of gypsophiles and gypsovags. Hint: They grow only in gypsum deposits like New Mexico's spectacular White Sands.

Armed with such arcane detail, I was able to take in the passing scenery with something of a connoisseur's eye as our little convoy descended from wind-carved sandstone buttes to the wide, flat Rio Grande Valley. Once we zipped up the ramp onto I-10, though, all bets were off. I was morally obligated to leave every lumbering semi in my dust, right?

I extended an arm straight up and waggled my fingers in farewell to the guys. Then I hit the gas. The stars must have aligned just right because not a single flashing red light appeared in my rearview mirror as I cruised along. Soon, very soon, I made out the purple smudge of the Franklin Mountains just west of El Paso.

Some moments later the city itself appeared in the distance. Downtown rose from the flatlands cut by the Rio Grande like steel-and-glass fingers reaching for the sky.

Since I'm not into cooking if there's a restaurant or fast-food joint within striking distance, I called my favorite Chinese place for a to-go order of dim sum, pork fried rice, and an extra crispy spring roll. I picked up the order and was sniffing the delicious scents emanating from the bag when I pulled into the entrance to my apartment complex. The place is typical Southwest, with lots of tile and adobe. Since it's close to Fort Bliss, it's also very military friendly. That makes for some lively Friday and Saturday nights around the pool.

As I toted my gear bag and dinner along the walkway to my apartment, I could see happy hour had already kicked off. Several couples were engaged in an energetic game of water volleyball. Others sprawled on loungers with plastic cups in hand. A portable iPod player belted out a golden oldie by Johnny Cash. I was humming along with the Man in Black and hoping to make it to my front door unnoticed when the wife of one of the instructors at Fort Bliss spotted me.

"Hey, Samantha!"

"Hi, Janie."

"We saw you on TV." She hooked an arm, waving me over. "Come tell us about this hit man you got crosswise with."

"Forget the hit man," her husband countered. "I want to hear about the reward."

I weighed the invitation against my half-formed plans for the evening. They included dinner in front of the TV while I did a week's worth of laundry and sorted through the junk mail that had piled up. A leisurely shower during which I would shampoo my hair and shave my legs in anticipation of Mitch's visit early tomorrow morning. A blissful night of sleep uninterrupted by Pen's snorts and snuffles.

As opposed to a sparkling pool and a friendly crowd.

No contest!

"I'll dump my stuff and change into my suit," I called back. "Pour me a cold one."

"You got it."

The dim sum and fried rice went into the fridge. My dusty boots and ABUs hit the bedroom floor. The clip still clinging haphazardly to my wind-whipped hair got tossed aside. I felt almost human again in my flip-flops and skimpy two-piece, with an old UNLV T-shirt as a cover up.

Several long, thirsty swallows of ice-cold Coors completed the transformation. Everyone poolside wanted the gory details. Not just about Duarte and his trophies. As I mentioned previously, drug wars and violence are pandemic along the border. The reward and Snoopy generated a good deal more interest among this mostly military crowd.

Discussion soon progressed from the robots's fuel consumption to possible battlefield applications. I was both relieved and pleased to have the crowd validate my gut instinct about Snoop's potential. Now all I had to do was demonstrate it, I reminded myself when I left the gang at the pool some hours later and flip-flopped back to may apartment.

That's when I spotted a figure dressed in dark clothes trying to jimmy open the sliding glass door to my patio. I stopped dead, gaping in surprise, then gave an indignant yelp.

"Hey! What the heck do you think . . . ?"

That's all I got out before he whirled and my stomach dropped like the proverbial stone.

CHAPTER FIVE

"CHARLIE?"

"Hi, babe."

My former, unlamented husband gave me an all-too-familiar grin. Half cocky, half pure sex. The curly black hair, laughing blue eyes, and broad chest that went with it weren't too shabby, either.

Charlie Spade still had one smokin' hot bod. All I needed was a single glance at his thigh-hugging jeans and the T-shirt stretched across the aforementioned chest to see he'd kept in shape since our quickie marriage and divorce.

Those wide shoulders and cheeky grin didn't do it for me anymore, though. I'd built up immunity to both even before I caught him with our over-endowed neighbor.

"When did you get into breaking and entering?" I demanded, hands on hips.

"I wasn't trying to get in. Just look in."

"Could've fooled me!"

"I rang the doorbell, Sam. You didn't answer, but the lights were on. I thought maybe you looked through the peephole, saw it was me, and went into hiding."

"Why would I hide from you?"

Dumb question, I realized as soon as the words were out. There was only one reason he would show up on my doorstep unannounced.

"You heard about the reward, didn't you?"

"Brenda did."

Brenda being our slutty ex-neighbor and Charlie's current wife.

"She saw your picture on TV. She said the photo made you look sort of bloated but . . ."

"She's one to talk!"

He skimmed a glance down my bikini-clad length. "But it looks to me like you've shed a few pounds."

Guess that's what chasing robots and other outlandish inventions in the desert heat will do for you. I appreciated the compliment but not the complimenter.

"If you made the trip from Vegas hoping for a cut of that reward, you can jump in whatever you're driving these days and head right back."

"The thing is, Sam, I'm in kind of a jam."

"Not my problem." I waved good-bye and breezed toward the door. "Adios, Carlos."

"Geez, Samantha." He dogged my heels. "We haven't seen each other in more than two years. Least you could do is invite me in for coffee or a beer or something."

I rolled my eyes. That's Charlie Spade in a nutshell.

Completely oblivious to the fact that the last time we were together in the same room he came perilously close to being gelded.

"Com'on, babe." While I keyed the door, he rubbed the back of his neck and let a little boy whine sneak into his voice. "It's a long stretch from Vegas to El Paso. One cup of coffee. That's all I'm asking for before you send me on my way."

"The 7-Eleven on the corner is open all night. You can get a cup there."

I closed the door in his face, or tried to. His foot wedged in the crack.

"Please, Sam." The whine evaporated, replaced by a desperate note. "I'm in over my head. You gotta help me climb out."

I didn't have to help him climb anywhere. I had a divorce decree to prove it. I started to remind him of our non-joined status when his expression stopped me cold. No question about it. The man was scared.

My conscience doesn't ping very often, but Charlie and I *had* exchanged bodily fluids two or three times a day during our first, heady weeks together. I couldn't turn the man away without at least letting him cry on my shoulder for a few minutes.

"Okay," I conceded with something less than graciousness. "One cup of coffee, then you hit the road."

I almost changed my mind once we were inside the apartment and he looked around, smirking.

"I see you're still not real big on dusting."

I could have informed him that I just returned from a week in the desert and hadn't had time to unpack, much less stir the accumulated dust. I would have been wasting my breath. As my former husband knows very well, comfortable and cluttered is a whole lot more my style than neat and tidy.

Which is why officer training school darn near killed me, by the way. Not the aerobics or the marching drills or all the classes on military history and strategy. Those I whizzed through. What almost did me in were the idiotic room inspections. Beds had to be made so tight you could bounce a quarter off the blanket. Shoes had to be precisely aligned. Bras had to be cupped, panties folded into two-inch squares, slips and camisoles . . .

Well, you get the picture. Not being the cupping or quarter-bouncing type, I conducted a special celebration when I finally pinned on my lieutenant's bars. Academy grads toss their hats in the air at graduation. I tossed my bras and panties.

They still get tossed. Onto chairs or floors or door handles. It's my way of expressing the non-military side of my personality. The tossing extends to other objects as well but I won't bore you with a detailed description of the items littering my apartment. Suffice it to say I'm very content in my surroundings.

"The coffeemaker's on the kitchen counter," I informed my ex. "The coffee's in the cupboard right above it. Why don't you get a pot perking while I change out of this bathing suit?"

"Hey, don't change on my account."

His eyes did the skimming thing again. Mine did another roll.

"Put the coffee on, Spade."

I went in the bedroom and shimmied out of the wet suit. The air conditioner was raising goose bumps all over, so I slipped into briefs, drawstring sweatpants that rode loose on my hips, and a red tank with a sequined Eiffel Tower—symbol of the Vegas casino where I used to work, not the French icon.

Charlie was sitting at the kitchen counter when I returned. He was playing with a stick of the Wrigley's Big Red gum he always has on him since he quit smoking. The uncharacteristic droop to his shoulders stirred a grudging sympathy.

"So what's the story?" I asked as I rounded the counter to retrieve two mugs from the cabinet. "What kind of hole did you dig yourself into?"

"I borrowed some money." He peeled back the foil paper, folded the gum, and popped it in. "The guy who loaned it to me wants it back. With interest."

"How much?"

"Fifteen thousand."

"Fifteen *thousand*!"

"Yeah," he said miserably. "I know."

I'd never seen him play anything steeper than the quarter slots during our brief marriage, but Vegas has a way of sneaking up on you.

"Gambling debts?"

"Doctor bills."

"But I thought . . ."

He has a good job, or did. With full medical coverage.

"Aren't you still working for Anderson Construction?"

"Yeah, but their insurance doesn't cover cosmetic surgery."

I stepped back, blinking in surprise, and conducted a quick head-to-toe.

"I probably shouldn't ask, but inquiring minds want to know. What did you have altered?"

"Not me. Brenda. Her back was hurting her something awful 'cause of all that weight she carried up front, so her doc recommended a breast reduction."

I couldn't contain myself. I didn't even try. This was too, too delicious. Planting my hands on the counter, I let loose with loud, raucous whoops.

"I know." Charlie popped his Big Red and gave me a sheepish smile. "Kind of ironic, isn't it."

"Kind of?"

I hooted for several more moments before sobering up enough for a thought to occur. You can't live and work in Vegas without becoming friends with at least one topless performer. I'd bummed around with several. Thus I knew breast surgery usually ran closer to five thousand than fifteen. When I mentioned as much to my ex, he nodded.

"Yeah, I know. But Brenda figured as long as she was going under the knife, she might as well get a tummy tuck and butt lift, too." His grin slipped out, cocky as ever. "I gotta tell you, Sam, the woman looks good. Really good."

"Just what an ex-wife wants to hear about the woman who got it on with her husband," I drawled.

Like Dr. Penelope England, Charles William Spade is immune to sarcasm. That's one of the traits I like best in both of them, dammit.

I didn't want to feel sorry for the dope. And God knows, I would have cheerfully consigned Brenda Baby to an eternity of backaches and sagging butt cheeks. Yet pity tugged at me when my former husband's grin faded and he stretched a hand across the counter to cover one of mine.

"Help me get the loan sharks off my back, Sam. Please."

"I wish I could, Charlie. Honestly. But this reward . . . I wasn't the one who took down number two on the FBI's Most Wanted list. I may not be able to claim any of the reward money."

"The news reports said you could."

"Yeah, well, there's an added complication. I was on duty at the time of the shooting. The military has all these rules about gratuities and gifts and such. A reward could fall into the same category."

"The shooting happened, like, three days ago. You haven't checked out these rules?"

"I was too busy checking out penalties for war crimes."

"Huh?"

I was in no mood to try and explain Snoopy's flesh-eating tendencies.

"Never mind. Look . . ." I hesitated, knowing I would kick myself for this in the morning. "If anything breaks on the reward, I'll do what I can to help you, okay?"

"Thanks, babe."

"You're welcome." I filled the two mugs and shoved one at him. "Now drink your coffee and hit the road."

He cradled the mug in both hands to blow away the steam. He had strong hands, I acknowledged reluctantly. Big and tanned, with blunt-tipped fingers and trimmed nails. He knew how to use them, too. We'd had some wild times in those first days and weeks and months. I remember once when we . . .

". . . on the couch?"

I jerked my gaze from his hands to his face. Heat crawled up my neck. Were my thoughts that obvious?

"What?"

"It's too late to hit the road. How about I spend what's left of the night on your couch? I'll leave first thing in the morning."

"No."

"Why not? What's the big deal?"

"Think a moment. How would you explain spending the night with your ex-wife to your current wife?"

"Geez, Sam. It's not like you and I are gonna jump into bed with each other."

"You got that right. Now finish your coffee and leave. I have plans for tomorrow morning that don't include you."

"We're just talking a few hours here."

"You are *not* spending the night, Charlie."

His blue eyes lost their spark. Shoulders slumping, he nodded. "All right."

Okay, okay! I know what you're thinking. I'm a spineless wimp. That's what I was thinking, too, as I stalked to the closet, retrieved a pillow and blanket, and threw them onto the sofa.

I went to bed too tired to shave my legs or shower off the chlorine from the pool. I sincerely regretted both omissions when I woke the next morning to the scent of yet another pot of coffee and the murmur of male voices.

Grimacing, I glanced at the digital clock beside my bed. Six twenty. Terrific! The one morning Mitch had to get off patrol early. Before I'd had time to send Charlie on his way or spiff myself up for a reunion.

I pulled on the tank and sweats I'd discarded last night and padded to the bathroom. The image that greeted me in the mirror produced a groan. But there wasn't much I could do about it at this point except splash water on my face, scrape the fuzz off my teeth, and drag a comb through my chlorinated hair.

I'm not a morning person to begin with, and the sight of my former husband and current lover sitting across from each other at my kitchen counter, shooting the breeze, didn't do much to brighten my day.

"Good morning," I mumbled, not real sure of the protocol for occasions like this.

"Hey, babe."

That came from Charlie. Mitch's greeting included a smile and the crinkly thing at the corners of his eyes I liked so much.

"'Morning, Samantha."

"I see you two have met."

Nodding, Mitch rose to pour me some coffee. He was in his Border Patrol greenies but had shed his utility belt. It was draped it on the back of his stool, along with his floppy brimmed boonie hat. I could see the effects of his long night in his face. Dark gold bristles were sprouting on his cheeks and chin. The squint lines framing his hazel eyes cut deeper than usual.

The first time I'd met Border Patrol Agent Jeff Mitchell, he'd reminded me a little of Charlie. Same approximate height, same broad shoulders, same ropy muscles. The resemblance didn't score him any brownie points at the time.

Only after I got to know him did I learn to appreciate the difference between a grown man and an overgrown adolescent. Mitch possesses an inbred sense of duty and a strength of character my ex has yet to develop. 'Course, he's almost ten years older and a century more experienced than Charlie. Maybe there's hope for Spade yet.

"You look tired," I observed as Mitch handed me a mug.

"I am."

The kiss he dropped on my mouth said just the opposite, however. I felt the sizzle all the way down to my bare toes and couldn't wait to send Charlie on his way. Easier to think than do, I soon learned.

"Your husband's been telling me about his problems," Mitch commented, hooking a hip on his bar stool while I propped my elbows on the countertop and cradled my coffee in both hands.

"*Ex*-husband."

I experienced an odd twinge as I stressed the point. Mitch is divorced, too. For almost four years now. Yet on the rare occasions he mentions his former spouse, he generally omits the prefix.

"I told Charlie I might be able to help him."

"You've got a spare fifteen thousand lying around?"

I wouldn't be surprised if he did. Mitch works long

hours and lives a pretty Spartan existence when not on duty. I've been trying to domesticate him. Even got him to spring for a leather sofa a few months back. We needed one big enough for us both to get horizontal. The rest of his place is still pretty bare, though.

"Mitch knows someone in Vegas," Charlie volunteered. "He says this guy might be able to ease some of the pressure on me."

I'd lived and worked in Vegas. I knew darn well that cold, hard cash was the only way to ease the kind of pressure he was talking about

"Right," I drawled. "And I've got this beachfront lot in Florida I'll sell you cheap."

Charlie wouldn't quite meet my eyes. Not a good sign, I knew, but I didn't say anything more until he finally departed. When the door closed behind him, I turned to Mitch.

"How much did you give him?"

"Just enough to keep his creditors from hammering spikes into his kneecaps until he comes up with the rest."

I chewed on my lower lip. I didn't really want a person or persons unknown to hammer a spike through Charlie's knees. Not anymore, anyway. It just didn't sit too well having Mitch contribute to the Brenda Boob Reduction Fund. Nor could I guarantee he'd ever see his investment again.

"Aside from acting like a total jerk most of the time, Spade's not all that bad," I said, frowning. "But it's anyone's guess when—or if—he'll pay you back."

"That's between him and me. Besides . . ."

His mouth curved in a lazy smile. Sliding a hand

into the waistband of my sweatpants, he tugged me into the V of his thighs.

"I consider the money well spent. It got rid of him, didn't it?"

My pulse skipped. Wishing to heck I'd forced myself to wield a razor last night, I hooked a prickly calf around his.

"True." I searched the tired lines carved into his face. "You sure you're up for this?"

Grinning, he tugged me closer. "What do you think?"

Whooo, boy! He was most definitely up for it.

So was I. Hunger sparked hot and sweet as I popped the buttons of his uniform shirt and dragged the tails free of his belt. Greedily, I slid my palms over soft cotton and hard muscle. His hands went to my hips, cupped my bottom. We were mouth to mouth and pelvis to pelvis when his cell phone pinged.

Groaning, I tried to distract him with a tongue-sucking kiss. The damned phone kept on pinging.

"Don't answer it!"

Despite my mutter, I knew I was wasting my breath. That inbred sense of duty I told you about is as much a part of Mitch as his sexy grin and gold-flecked eyes. So I didn't get *too* bent out of shape when he reached for the phone clipped to his utility belt.

I expected him to check caller ID and, if the gods were merciful, let the call go to voice mail. I didn't expect his brows to snap together and his expression to turn all hard and stony.

"I have to take this."

I disengaged, wondering why the tendons in his neck

had knotted. He flipped up the lid but didn't say hello. Didn't identify himself. Just snarled into the speaker.

"You know better than to call me at this number."

He turned away, his entire body rigid. I hitched my sweatpants higher and tried to decide whether to stay where I was or give him some privacy. His next words killed my internal debate.

"Jesus, Margo! How could you let this happen?"

My eyes popped. What the heck was this? Former Spouse Week? First Charlie Spade shows up on my doorstep. Now Mitch's wife—*ex*-wife—calls out of the blue. Not being particularly shy or discreet, I listened with unabashed curiosity to the terse, one-sided dialogue that followed.

"Yes . . . No . . . I will." His knuckles went white. "I said I will!"

The cell phone snapped shut. When my tough, macho Border Patrol agent turned to face me, the look in his eyes shoved my breath back down my throat.

"It's Jenny."

Oh, God! The teenage daughter Mitch had seen only twice in the past four years. The daughter he'd shipped off to Seattle with her mother for their own protection. The daughter some lowlife named Rafael Mendoza had made vicious, unspeakable threats against.

"What . . . ?" I couldn't breathe, could barely speak. "What about Jenny?"

"She's run away."

CHAPTER SIX

MY delicious anticipation of long hours spent in and out of bed with my handsome Border Patrol agent evaporated on the spot.

"Is Margo sure Jenny's run off?" I asked with a catch in my throat.

Mitch didn't talk much about the circumstances that had sent his daughter and her mother out of his life. He'd told me enough, however, for dread to hover front and center in my mind until he nodded.

"Jen left a note. Said she's tired of Margo coming down on her all the time. Informed her mother that she's going to hang with a friend for a while. Someone Margo doesn't know." He scraped a hand over his jaw. "I have to fly up there, Samantha. I have to make sure she's safe."

"Of course. Want me to check flight schedules while you call your boss?"

"Thanks."

He had his cell phone to his ear before I unzipped the laptop I'd deposited last night on the glass-topped dining table that did double duty as my desk. I powered up, eavesdropping shamelessly while I waited for the icons to blossom on my MacBook. Mitch's boss must have known the circumstances behind his separation from his only child. He agreed to put the Border Patrol agent on leave with minimal discussion of the reason for it.

I found a Southwest flight departing El Paso in a little over two hours. After a quick input of Mitch's credit card number, he was booked.

"I need to change and get my vehicle back to the yard," he said, his mind clearly already at twenty thousand feet and winging north. "Mind picking me up at the station and dropping me off at the airport?"

"No problem. I'll get dressed and meet you there."

He strapped on his utility belt with its various accoutrements, dropped a quick kiss on my nose, and departed.

With the absence of the two well-built males who'd occupied it, my tiny apartment seemed suddenly empty and sterile. Except for the scattered magazines and mail, of course, and the dust motes floating on the sunbeams that slanted through the windows.

I swallowed a slug of coffee and carried the mug with me into the bedroom. My sweatpants and tank joined the ABUs on the floor. I shimmied into jeans, a once-blue USAF T-shirt, and flip-flops before giving my hair another few swipes with a brush. Didn't help. The chlorine had done a real number on it. I crammed on a Texas Rangers baseball cap, pulled the springy auburn mass through the back opening, and headed out.

The Ysleta Border Patrol Station consists of a cluster of stucco buildings in what was once flat farmland. The station's fenced yard was large enough to house a fleet of vehicles, most of which were out on patrol when I pulled up at the entry point.

The Border Patrol's primary mission used to be to deter illegals and smugglers. After 9/11, priority shifted to apprehending terrorists attempting to enter the United States. Not an easy task, as I've learned during my association with Mitch these past months. On a typical day, Customs and Border Patrol personnel process some 1.13 million passengers and pedestrians entering the U.S.; 70,000 truck, rail, and sea containers; and $88 million in fees, duties, and tariffs. They also apprehend 2,400 folks and seize more than 7,000 pounds of narcotics.

Daily!

The statistics went a long way to explaining the tired lines cut into Mitch's face when he slid into the convertible's passenger seat. Worry for his daughter explained the rest. I could have told him most teenage girls felt obligated to rebel against their mothers on a more or less regular basis. I certainly did. Then again, I didn't have a father on the bad side of a vicious criminal.

"Call me when you get to Seattle," I made him promise after we'd pulled up at the airport.

Nodding, he gave me a semi-distracted kiss before levering out of the convertible. I watched him disappear inside the terminal. Then I cut into the airport traffic stream and tried to decide what to do with the rest of my day.

The mall beckoned. Ten days out at Dry Springs with my team always left me with an insatiable Macy's craving. Unfortunately, it also left me with piles of test reports to synthesize and a stack of new submissions to review. I supposed I could go out to Fort Bliss and use the quiet hours of a Saturday morning to make a dent in the stack.

Or I could craft a carefully worded email to Dr. J inquiring about the propriety of accepting the reward. Macy's would certainly be a lot more fun with a big chunk of change jingling in my pockets.

Hmmm. Tough choice. Shopping with my present limited resources. Or waiting until I could enjoy a more extravagant incursion.

Just about everyone who knows me will confirm I'm not into delayed gratification. Or hard logic. Took me all of ten seconds to decide this was just too pretty a morning to be stuck in an office building (as opposed to an enclosed, windowless mall).

Since I was already headed north toward the base and the mall lay in the opposite direction, I had to cut across two lanes of traffic to exit Airport Road. The drivers behind me didn't take kindly to my emergency maneuvers. One laid on his horn. Another flipped me the bird. I mouthed an apology to the rearview mirror but felt somewhat vindicated when a gray Chevy two cars back executed the same abrupt exit.

Five minutes later my cell phone warbled out a slightly X-rated version of "The Eyes of Texas" and I had to change directions again. Very reluctantly, I might add. Charlie, it turns out, hadn't even reached the outskirts of town before his pickup wheezed and died. He'd had it towed to a Ford dealership but was stuck in El Paso until a part got shipped in.

"Damned part's manufactured in Singapore or India or someplace like that," he groused when I pulled into the dealership and he folded his long length into the Sebring. "They said they couldn't get one in until Tuesday."

"I hope you don't think you're going to stay at my place until then," I huffed. "I'll take you to a motel but that's as far as we go."

"Com'on, Sam. I can't afford three nights in a motel."

"I beg to differ. Didn't Mitch just loan you a thousand dollars?"

"I wired that to Brenda before I broke down. She used to work for the guy we borrowed from, so she knew just where to . . ."

"Wait a minute. She worked for the Mob?"

"She didn't know Richie was in the business."

"Yeah, right."

The cynical remark rolled off his Teflon-coated conscience. Shrugging, he popped in a stick of Big Red. "Brenda and me thought Rich might be more agreeable if she took the thousand in and asked for an extension."

Especially with her newly refurbished boobs and butt, I thought nastily. I managed to bite back that comment but couldn't refrain from an acid reminder.

"Your problems are *not* my concern, buddy boy."

"You say that, but you gotta think of the fallout if Brenda doesn't talk Richie into another grace period."

"Fallout?"

"You already made the news with this severed head

thing. I turn up dead, too, and the cops are gonna wonder if there's a connection."

"Dammit, Charlie, I don't appreciate being dragged into your mess."

"I know, babe."

That little boy whine seeped into his voice. I couldn't believe I used to think it was cute. Now it made my lips pull back.

"I'm sorry, Sam. I really am. Just put me up until they fix my truck. Soon's they do, I'm out of here. I promise."

I drummed my fingers on the steering wheel and weighed the options. I could leave him here at the dealership. Or dump him at the nearest motel with best wishes for a nice life. Or . . .

Or if I was really, really honest, I might be forced to admit Charlie did me a favor when he got it on with Brenda Baby. I didn't think so at the time, of course. But catching him in the act riled me so much I chucked him along with my dead-end job and marched into an Air Force recruiter's office. And despite my own and my entire family's expectations to the contrary, I'm still in uniform and actually doing something productive with my life.

I wasn't about to share these profound revelations with Charlie, however. Instead, I merely sighed and put the car in gear.

"Okay, okay. But you stay at my place *only* until Tuesday. If the part's not in by then, you sleep on the dealer's couch instead of mine."

* * *

WISH I could tell you Charlie was my only annoying visitor that weekend.

No such luck. When I pulled into my assigned parking space at my apartment complex, a car door opened two slots over. I was barely out of the convertible before a thin, fox-faced type in a shiny green suit, white shirt, and a string tie hurried over.

"Lieutenant Spade?"

I had no intention of confirming my identity until I found out who he was and what he wanted.

Charlie was every bit as gun-shy. With good reason! He was the one with the Mob after him. "Who wants to know?" he asked suspiciously.

"My name's Nowatny. Jim Nowatny." Fox Face palmed a card in my direction. "I believe your brother, Don, spoke to you about me, Lieutenant."

Recognition dawned. "You're the lawyer who got Don out of paying back taxes."

I hadn't intended it as a compliment but Nowatny preened. "That's right. Saved him close to twenty thousand."

Charlie's blue eyes lit up. The light blinked out again when I pointed out that those savings were all on paper. Except for Lawyer Nowatny's hefty fee, of course.

"Donny had to fork that over," I told my disappointed ex as we retreated toward my apartment.

"This is different." Nowatny dogged our heels. "I would take your case on a contingency basis. You don't get paid, I don't get paid."

"I don't have a case. Besides, your card lists an address in California. Are you even licensed to practice in Texas?"

"No, but I have a colleague who is."

Surprise, surprise. I could visualize his colleague's office. Two musty rooms in some strip mall down close to the Rio Grande, the better to snare clients coming over or being escorted back across the border.

"Sorry, I don't need legal representation."

"Yeah, babe, you do."

Leave it to Charlie to add his one and a half cent's worth.

"You said this agency you work for has all kinds of rules and regulations. They might get in the way of you collecting your fair share of the reward. I bet this guy . . . What's your name again?"

"Nowatny. Jim Nowatny."

"I bet Jim here could help you cut through the red tape."

I had a momentary vision of Fox Face descending on poor, unsuspecting Dr. J. Shuddering, I keyed my front door.

"Thanks, but no thanks. I'll work this out myself."

I shut the door firmly in Nowatny's face. Fished my cell phone out of my purse. Started counting. "One thousand one, one thousand two, one thousand . . ."

"What are you doing?" Charlie asked curiously.

"Seeing how long it takes the ambulance chaser outside to get Don to call me."

I resumed counting and got all the way to seventeen seconds before "The Eyes of Texas" belted out. Charlie broke out in a grin at the irreverent first stanza. Halfway through the second, he got impatient.

"Aren't you going to answer it?"

"Nope."

I let the call go to voice mail and put the phone to my ear. My mouth twisting sardonically, I listened to Don's attempt to come on all big-brotherly.

"You need to protect your interests, Sam. Make sure those other guys don't stiff you out of your share of the reward. Talk to Nowatny. Let him work this for you."

"No way in hell," I muttered.

THE voice mails piled up after that. Lawyer Nowatny. Don again. My mother. My cousin Deb, who'd evidently used Fox Face's legal expertise to resolve the little matter of a false worker's comp claim. Cub Reporter DeWayne, hoping to follow up on his big news break. My uncle Alex, who I hadn't heard from in ten years but wanted to congratulate me on hitting the jackpot, and oh, by the way, could I float him a small loan to cover the cost of the backyard in-ground pool his kids were hassling him about? The aboveground just wasn't hacking it anymore.

I got so tired of it all that I didn't bother to check caller ID when the phone rang late that afternoon. But the first chord's of Mitch's special ringtone had me grabbing for the instrument.

"What's the word on Jenny?" I asked anxiously.

"I found her."

I didn't ask how he'd accomplished that so quickly. As I've learned from my encounters with law enforcement types, they have access to sources not available to ordinary mortals. They also tend to close ranks. I've seen the steel jaws snap shut more than once, leaving me on the outside looking in. Mitch is better than most of his ilk. He'll tell me what he can, when he can. I didn't need to hear the nuts and bolts right now, though. Just knowing his daughter was safe relieved the worst of my fears.

His, too. I could hear it in his voice—along with a fair amount of exasperation. "She didn't want to go home. Says her mother just doesn't get it. "

"Think the two of them can work things out?"

"They have to. I promised to stay another couple of days and referee. I want the time with Jenny, but negotiating with Margo is going to max out my fun meter," he admitted wryly. "Twenty minutes with her and I was biting my tongue so hard I tasted blood."

That relieved a lesser worry. I hadn't really expected sparks to reignite when he connected with his ex again, but you never now about these things.

"Speaking of having to bite your tongue . . ."

My glance went to the shimmering turquoise pool visible through the sliding glass doors. *My* ex lay stretched out on a lounger, shirtless, balancing a beer bottle on his navel while he scarfed down the pizza he'd cajoled me into ordering. The jerk was soaking up rays as though he didn't have a care in the world.

"Charlie's truck died on his way out of town," I told Mitch. "He's here, mooching off me until they fly in a part from Indonesia or somewhere."

"Uh-oh."

"Uh-oh is right. If he mentions Brenda's boob reduction one more time, he might not make it back to Vegas with all *his* working parts."

"We'll trade horror stories when I get home."

The smile in Mitch's voice told me he wasn't worried about sparks reigniting, either. That's the great thing about falling for a guy with smarts and maturity. He doesn't sweat the small stuff. Although . . .

I might not have bridled at a *teeny* show of jealousy before he murmured his standard good-bye.

"So I'll see you when I see you."

"See you when I see you," I echoed.

I disconnected, missing Mitch and wondering what the heck I would do with Charlie for the next few days. He could only float and drink for so long, and I really did need to get caught up on some things

Luckily, inspiration came some hours later via another phone call, this one from Pen. "I know you said you weren't interested in attending the quarterly meeting of Scientists Against Biospheric Exploitation with me, Samantha, but our guest speaker had to cancel and I'm on the agenda instead. I'm going to talk about the silicon-wrapped carbon sensor we evaluated. The science wasn't quite there yet, but the theory behind it holds great promise."

I remembered that gizmo. All too well. Damned thing was supposed to measure carbon dioxide levels in a variety of extreme environments and transmit a warning signal when they reached danger levels. Need I say that it failed to perform as promised? Or that the test gave me the headache from hell?

"Sorry, Pen. I've got too much to do tomorrow."

"Are you sure? The Smokehouse is catering supper after the lecture," she added slyly.

Damn! The woman knows me too well. Carbon dioxide levels left me cold. Ribs dripping with the Smokehouse's secret sauce had me salivating on the spot.

I itched to ask how Scientists Against Biospheric Exploitation could square their rigid anti-emission standards with meat charred over nasty, smoke-spewing charcoal but knew better than to open that door. Pen's explanation would leave me numb. So would tomorrow afternoon's lecture. I can take her learned discourse in small doses. Two hours' worth would roll my eyes back in my head.

A devious thought snuck in. I love a messy, dripping rack of ribs. And unless Charlie's changed dramatically since our divorce, he inhales them whole.

My glance shot to the sliding glass doors again. Charlie was downing his third—fourth?—beer. A Doritos bag lay crumpled beside the empty pizza carton. At this rate, he'd clean me out of both food and funds before he hit the road again.

"I have a guest visiting who might be interested in attending the meeting with you, Pen."

Especially if I told him there were ribs involved.

"Can I call you back in a few minutes?"

"By all means."

SO call me evil. Immoral. Depraved.

I'm not ashamed to admit I felt nothing but glee when Pen drove up the following afternoon and I escorted Charlie out to her car to make the introductions. He did a double take when he took in her sturdy sandals and multilayers of shapeless linen. A third take when he spotted the long back feather spearing through her bun.

"I . . . Er . . ."

He threw me a helpless look. I ignored it.

"Have fun, you two."

I slammed the car door before he could escape and watched them drive off.

CHARLIE got even with me the next day. Big time. Although it wasn't *totally* his fault he set fire to the building that houses FST-3's home offices.

I should have known better than to take him to work with me. But it was either that or give him a key to my apartment. I didn't mind him loafing around the place but wasn't all that anxious to have him poking through my stuff. I also nursed this secret hope he might buddy up with Sergeant Cassidy and spend the rest of his enforced stay in El Paso with his new pal.

Thus I poked him in the shoulder at oh-dark-thirty Monday morning.

"Up and at 'em, Charlie."

"Huh?"

"I have to go to work. I thought you might want to come along and see what I do."

Bleary eyed, he blinked several times. "What time is it?"

"Almost six thirty."

"In the *morning*?"

"Com'on, you hit the shower and get dressed. I'll make coffee."

When he emerged I shoved a travel mug and a toasted bagel at him. "You'll have to eat it on the way."

I crammed on my patrol cap and slung my purse strap over my shoulder. Charlie's brows lifted as his gaze skimmed from my cap to my combat boots.

"That's some change from your last work uniform, babe."

"No kidding."

My previous duty uniform consisted of fishnet stockings, a flounced miniskirt, ruffled panties, and an off-the-shoulder peasant blouse. *Way* off the shoulder. Some male's fantasized vision of what a Parisian cocktail waitress should sashay around in. Now I clump around in boots and ABUs. That kind of uniform change takes a considerable psychological adjustment.

"So how do you like being a soldier?" Charlie asked as I shooed him out the door.

"Soldiers are Army. I'm Air Force."

"So how do you like it?"

Tough question. To tell the truth, officer training school was a severe shock to my psyche. Convinced I'd made the worst mistake in a life already riddled with errors in judgment, I almost quit several times. Each time, the stubborn streak my mother claims I was born with would kick in.

Same with my first months in uniform. Talk about your fish out of water! If Dr. J hadn't been as new to DARPA as I was myself, I'm sure I would have been shown the door. But he suffered through the first year with me as I slowly got the hang of things.

FST-3 is the real reason I've stuck it out this long.

I don't want to get all mushy here but... Well...
There's really something to this brotherhood-of-arms
business. Even among REMFs. That's the short version
of a less-than-polite term for rear echelon mother f...
Er, you get the picture. My team and I don't tote sub-
machine guns or strap ourselves into the cockpit of an
F-22. But each of us believes deep down in our hearts
that we're actually contributing to the safety and security of our nation by testing items that might someday
improve the capability of our troops in combat. Why
the heck else would we spend weeks out at Dry Springs,
with only each other for company?

Sounds corny, I know. Definitely not something I
wanted to articulate to Charlie at this ungodly hour of
the morning. Instead, I shrugged and hooked on my
seat belt.

"The Air Force and I have our occasional differ-
ences," I said with magnificent understatement. "I like
being in charge, though."

Grinning, Charlie folded a stick of Big Red into his
mouth. "You always did, babe."

I was still trying to decide how to take that when we
drove through the gates of Fort Bliss.

Don't be fooled by the name. Bliss refers to the individual the fort was named for, not necessarily the activi-
ties that take place here every day. At various points in
its history Fort Bliss served as an infantry outpost, a cavalry post, and an airfield for the Army's early aviation
efforts. It's since grown into a major training, mobiliza-

tion, and deployment center, with more than a million acres of test range straddling the Texas/New Mexico border. That makes it bigger than the state of Rhode Island.

And twice as busy! At any hour of the day or night there are live-fire exercises going on out on the range, troops assembling in the mobilization center, and thousands of military and civilian personnel going about their business—including my team of dedicated professionals.

FST-3 occupies a suite of offices in the historic section of the post. Our '30s-era building looks old and interesting on the outside. Inside it's just old. Various post commanders have eked out precious maintenance dollars for upkeep and renovation over the years. The overhead pipes are now concealed by acoustical tile and the johns flush on a more or less regular basis, but the wooden floors still creak and the HVAC system can't take the strain of a hot summer day in West Texas. I've brought this to the deputy post commander's attention on several occasions, along with repeated requests for more office space. Like Dr. J, Colonel Roberts also takes a loooong time to return my calls.

Despite my complaints, though, ten days out at Chuville always makes our Depression-era building seem like the height of luxury. This morning was no exception. I gazed fondly at the two-story wooden edifice as I angled the Sebring into the parking lot across the street.

My assigned parking space is close to a side entrance but I walked Charlie around to the front of the building to sign him in and get a visitor's pass. Security on post has tightened in response to world conditions. All of us on FST-3 heartily concur with the more stringent controls. Especially since they also help deter attacks by disgruntled inventors whose babies we've rejected. No small consideration when you consider some of the nuts we've dealt with.

My plan to keep Charlie busy and out of my hair appeared to work when I introduced him to Sergeant Cassidy at our regular morning confab. My whole team crams into my cubbyhole of an office at the start of each workday to review the status of ongoing projects and evaluate new submissions for possible field tests. Some of those submissions are so out there we groan and/or howl with laughter. Or in Pen's case, whinny like a bee-stung mare.

This morning was no different. We had the preliminary reports from our on-site tests to review and a stack of new submissions. I eyed the pile, sighed, and put off the inevitable long enough to introduce Charlie. He gave Pen a wary nod. Blinked at the neon image of Bobby Fischer on Dennis O'Reilly's perpetual black T-shirt. Offered a hesitant hand to Rocky, who'd attired himself for our return to civilization in a white short-sleeved shirt, black tie, and pale blue pinstriped seersucker slacks.

As I'd hoped, Charlie and Noel recognized kindred spirits in each other. So much so that when Noel requested two hours for mandatory physical fitness training, he suggested he take Charlie to the gym with him. I gave him four hours. Two would barely break Noel out in a sweat. He racks up his PT points by doing, oh, a thousand or so sit-ups before taking every machine at the gym to the max. And four hours would keep Charlie out of the way while I waded through the piles on my desk.

"How about you check on whether you can accept the reward while we're at the gym?" my ex asked hopefully. When Noel added his endorsement, I promised to call the Fort Bliss legal office. Better to start at this level and get a military lawyer's input before approaching the scientific properties and patent attorneys at headquarters.

I made the call and set up an appointment for three that afternoon. When Charlie and Noel returned from the gym they were disappointed I didn't have an answer. Dennis O'Reilly assuaged their disappointment by taking them to lunch at Papa Leone's, his favorite Italian place. Then, much to the amazement of the rest of the team, my big, brawny ex clicked with our nervous little test engineer.

I can't imagine two more dissimilar personalities. Or what in the *heck* they would have in common. Yet when I poked my head into Rocky's cubicle to see what they were up to, there was Dr. Brian Balboa attempting to explain in layman's terms a small square object the inventor had labeled an Amorphic Cube. According to the teenage tinkerer who put it together, his cube could assume any shape with the flick of a switch.

Clearly intrigued with the concept, Charlie glanced up at me. "Have you seen this thingamajig, Sam?"

"I read the specs." Mostly. "Haven't seen it in operation yet."

"Rocky here says it can go flat as a dime or sprout wings or maybe even shape itself into a spare part for a tank or Humvee."

The speculative look in his eyes told me exactly what he was thinking. I have to admit I was thinking the same thing. But I resisted the temptation to beg Rocky to morph the cube into a spare part for a Ford F-150 that would whisk Charlie Spade out of my life again.

"I ran a preliminary test on the device to see if it merited a full field evaluation," Rocky informed us both. "The results were disappointing."

"Yeah?" Charlie worked his Big Red and turned the cube over and over in his hands. "Disappointing how?"

Struggling to explain in a way he—and I—would understand, Rocky held up a wand-type device.

"The signals from this control unit travel only a short distance. We would have to boost their power considerably to make the Amorphic Cube viable for battlefield conditions."

"Hey, maybe I could help with that. I'm pretty good at fiddling around with video game controls."

Hastily, I intervened. "That isn't a game unit. It's a highly sophisticated device submitted for evaluation by the Department of Defense."

"Yeah, but I tried this trick I know on one of my game controls when it started to die on me. All I had to do to power up the signal was . . ."

"Listen to me, Charlie," I said sternly. "We don't do 'tricks.' We're required to adhere to strict test protocols."

Rocky's brows soared. Ignoring his look of utter

amazement at hearing me echo the strictures he'd preached at me so often, I asked him to step into my office for a minute.

"I need you to interpret some of the language in your draft report on Snoopy SNFIR."

I've made some serious errors in judgment in my life. Hitting the Tunnel of Love Drive Thru wedding chapel with Charlie Spade was one. Leaving him alone with that little gadget was another.

He's dumb, but not stupid. He also has a lively sense of curiosity. And, as he'd pointed out, he's really good with video games. So I should have anticipated that he would jimmy open the cube's control unit, insert a tiny strip of silver-backed chewing gum paper, and plug the unit into an electrical outlet.

What neither of us anticipated were the sparks that spewed from the socket mere moments later.

"Holy crap!"

His startled shout brought my entire team on the run. To our dismay, we discovered that Charlie's homemade booster had ignited an electrical fire that now raced up our '30s-era wiring.

CHAPTER SEVEN

I grabbed the closest extinguisher and aimed foam at the sparking flames. Noel ripped some fiberboard away with his bare hands so the suppressant could get to the shorting wires. Rocky and Charlie scrambled to shove the furniture aside. Our combined efforts kept the papers and assorted objects in Rocky's cubicle from incinerating. Unfortunately, we weren't quick enough to keep the overhead sprinklers from going off.

We got the flames out before the fire department responded, but when I surveyed all those waterlogged computers, I had to forcibly restrain myself from doing something very un-officerish. Like indulging in a healthy bout of hysterics. Or slinking out the back door. Or deflecting the evil looks aimed at me by the other occupants of the building by reminding them that the wiring had probably come in with Prohibition.

That's the thing about being in charge, though. No hysteria or slinking or finger-pointing allowed. You have to suck it up and take full responsibility for the actions of your people. Or in this case, your ex-husband.

Thank God I'd followed proper procedures and checked Charlie in at the security checkpoint. *And* had one of the team members escort him in and out of our area. *And* made sure he hadn't had access to sensitive information. The Farmer Farnsworths of the world generally use off-the-shelf components to create their masterpieces, but how they assemble the components is proprietary information. Even with those safeguards, I cringed at the thought of explaining Charlie to the deputy post commander. And—big gulp!—Dr. J.

I cringed even more when I remembered the excruciating process I went through after the fire out at the test site some months ago. I'd had to complete reams of reports detailing the loss and damage to government property. Headquarters even sent a senior officer out to Texas to conduct an official inquiry. This was worse, though. Much worse. Since this was an Army-maintained facility, I would have *two* sets of regulations to slog through.

"Okay, folks," I said when the fire response team finally departed. "Let's clean up this mess and assess the damage."

We got to it, wielding mops and roll after roll of paper towels as we worked our way methodically down our end of the hall. To my infinite relief, the gizmos and gadgets entrusted to my sacred care seemed to have survived intact. Snoopy SNFIR was safe and dry in his packing crate. Big whew there. Last thing I needed was for an irate Farmer F. to call another news conference and rake us over the coals again. And Charlie had managed to keep the shape-shifting cube from getting doused by the sprinklers.

As mentioned, our computers took severe hits. So did a good many personal items like framed photos, books, several cell phones, and the iPods everyone seemed to have in their purse or pocket. Each loss gave rise to mutters or groans. The worst came from Dennis O'Reilly when he spotted the now-indecipherable signature on his autographed poster of chess great Garry Kasparov.

"Oh, no!"

We gathered around, trying to comfort him as his eyes blurred with tears behind his thick lenses.

"I'll brew you some tea," Pen said consolingly. "My peppermint, lemon balm, and goji berry blend is specially designed to lift spirits."

Our coffeepot had shorted out, as had the vending machine that provided my usual noontime sustenance. But to Pen's delight and the collective dismay of the rest of us, airtight glass canisters had protected her assortment of herbal teas. She hurried off to secure hot water from the undamaged break room at the other end of the hall and missed Dennis's agonized look.

"What's a goji berry?"

None of the rest of us had a clue but were all secretly relieved he would to be the one to find out and not us.

I had formulated a preliminary estimate of the damage

when we finally shut down for the day. It was well past seven by then. Rush-hour traffic had dwindled to a trickle. A double-edged sword, in my opinion. Without the mass exodus to constrain me I had even more trouble than usual sticking to the post's absurd twenty-five-mile-per-hour speed limit. My left foot thumped the floor mat impatiently. My right hit the brake, the accelerator, the brake again.

Charlie was too chagrined by his part in the drama—or too used to my predilection for speed—to comment until we'd cleared the gate. Then his gaze strayed to the fast-food joints whizzing past the windows and he cleared his throat.

"It's been a while since lunch."

"Hey, you ate at Papa Leone's. I grabbed a Coke and peanut butter crackers from the vending machines. Before you killed them," I added nastily.

He ignored the snide reminder. "Then you need a good dinner. How does Mexican sound?"

"Are you treating?"

"You know I'm short on funds." He actually managed to look hurt. "And I still have to get my truck out of hock tomorrow."

"I hope to God it's ready tomorrow! Did you call to check the status?" I groaned at his sheepish expression. "Charlieeeee."

"Sorry, babe. All that excitement at your office . . . I forgot to call."

"Try now. Maybe the service department stays open past seven."

It didn't. Resigned, I steered through the early evening traffic. The spectacular view of the Franklin Mountains bathed in shades of pink and orange usually lifted my spirits. Not tonight. All I could think of were the regulations and reports I would have to slog through tomorrow.

"There's a good Mexican restaurant close to my place. It's border cuisine," I warned. "Might be spicier than you're used to."

Actually, Dos Lobos offered patrons a choice between green and red sauce. One was supposed to be milder than the other depending on that year's chili crop, but both broke me out in a sweat.

"No problem," Charlie boasted. "I can handle anything they throw at me."

After that bit of braggadocio I could hardly wait for his reaction when he scooped a tortilla chip into the salsa. It wasn't long in coming. One crunch had his eyes bugging almost out of his head.

"Omigod!"

Frantically fanning his mouth, he snatched up his glass. When he chugged all of his water and half of mine, I smiled for the first time that day.

"I thought you could handle it, tough guy?"

Sweat beaded on his forehead. Tears leaked from the corners of his eyes. "I thought I could, too," he croaked.

For reasons I've yet to understand, Charlie's acute agony erased much of the animosity I'd felt for him since his sudden reappearance in my life. I was almost sorry for the guy as he slumped against the back of the booth.

"Jesus, Sam. You eat here often?"

"Often enough. Mitch likes their sour cream enchiladas."

He scrubbed his eyes with his napkin and gave me a watery look over the bunched paper. "So what's the story with you and Mitch? You two serious?"

"We haven't stopped to analyze things," I replied with a shrug. "I like him. He likes me. That's enough for both of us right now."

And the sex was really, really good. I nibbled on a chip, hoping the referee thing went well so Mitch could jump on a plane soon. First, though, I had to get rid of Charlie.

I was thinking metaphorically at that moment. Honestly!

I had no idea a shadowy figure was going to lunge out of the darkness when we got back to my apartment and almost do the job for me.

Charlie saw him first. Startled, he stumbled back. "What the . . . ?"

He didn't stumble far or fast enough. Something long and straight swung in a vicious arc and slammed into his gut. He doubled over, grunting in pain, and dropped to his knees.

The unexpected assault had shocked me into immobility for several critical seconds. Just long enough for Charlie's attacker to swing in my direction. Hefting what I now saw was a length of pipe, he snarled at me.

"Get in the car!"

Mitch's advice for any woman caught in this kind of

nightmare slashed through my stunned surprise. *Scream your head off, and for God's sake, don't get into an attacker's vehicle if you can help it.* So I screamed my head off.

"Help! Somebody! Anybody!"

Still bellowing, I dodged around the Sebring's rear end. The pipe-wielding bastard followed. His weapon sliced through the air. He missed me by inches and crunched the Sebring's fender instead. The taillights shattered on his next swing.

For God's sake! Where were all the pool paddlers and beer guzzlers when you needed them? I looked around frantically for something to use as a weapon or a shield to blunt the force of that lethal pipe. I'd just about given up hope when the front door of the apartment across from mine flew open.

"Samantha? That you?"

Almost sobbing with relief, I spied my neighbor. Tony's day job was as an instructor at the Patriot missile school on post. Nights he moonlighted as a bouncer at a local strip joint.

"Tony! Help!"

He charged down the sidewalk. My attacker swung around, got a good look at the muscled-up new threat, and dropped the pipe. It was still clanging against the asphalt when the bastard leaped into a car parked two slots away.

He'd keyed the ignition and had shoved his vehicle into reverse before I could scoop up his weapon. I managed to get in one good lick, though. I slammed the pipe into the driver's side door and heard the satisfying crunch of metal on metal before he tore off, tires squealing.

"My car keys are in the house!" Tony shouted as he sprinted into the parking lot. "Toss me yours and I'll follow this joker."

I'd dropped the key ring in my purse. By the time I rooted through the jumble and fished it out, our attacker was long gone, so I tossed him my cell phone instead.

"Call nine-one-one."

While Tony stabbed at the buttons, I knelt beside my ex. Charlie was on all fours, clutching his middle and wheezing like an asthmatic moose.

"Are you okay?"

His lips curled back in a snarl. "Do I . . . look . . . okay?"

"Don't move. You might have a cracked rib."

"Feels more . . . like three."

Oh, no! The horrific vision of my former spouse with his midsection taped and camped out for the foreseeable future on my sofa leaped into my head. It leaped out again when we heard another squeal of tires. All three of us froze as headlights speared through the parking area.

For a terrifying moment I thought our attacker had returned. With the headlights blinding me, I couldn't see the interior of the vehicle that screeched to a halt just yards away. But I saw Tony scoop up the pipe and race toward the car to give as good as Charlie had gotten. My heart in my throat, I watched him yank open the driver's door. Then a shrill and very feminine shriek split the night air.

"Don't hurt me! We'll pay it back! I swear!"

Charlie jerked upright. Relief and delight poured out of him in palpable waves. "Brenda?"

A head topped by piles of bottle-blond hair poked out of the car. A disgustingly svelte size six followed.

"Snoogs?"

I sank back on my heels. Could this day *get* any more bizarre?

"Oh, Snoogs!" Elbowing me aside, my former neighbor and one-time best friend dropped to her knees and cradled Charlie in her arms. "What did Richie's goon do to you?"

"Was . . . that who . . . it was?"

She nodded, her eyes swimming with tears and a half a pound of mascara. "Richie came to the Four Queens."

Guess I should mention here that Brenda also works in a casino. She's a blackjack dealer. No short skirts or ruffled panties for her. Just black slacks and a neat white blouse with garters on the sleeves. But all the woman had to do was lean over the table to totally distract the players. The male players, anyway. I couldn't help wondering what casino management thought of her newly redefined silhouette as she sobbed to Charlie.

"I wasn't at work when he asked about you. Harry told him you'd driven over to El Paso. The idiot let drop that your ex had hit it big."

Yeah, I thought sardonically. And what idiot told Harry?

"He said you were going to borrow the fifteen grand from Sam," Brenda got out through her watery sniffles. "I guess . . . I guess Richie figured he'd better make sure you didn't take off without paying."

She lifted her tear- and mascara-streaked face and glared at me.

"This is all your fault, Sam."

"Mine?"

"I wouldn't have had surgery if Charlie hadn't joked about how I made, like, three of you."

My ex/her current tried desperately to extricate himself from the quagmire. "I've told you a hundred times! I meant that as compliment, Bren."

Clearly unconvinced, she sniffed. I sniffed, too. I can't claim anything close to Brenda's former proportions, but I'm not totally deficient in the cup-size department.

I could have saved my breath. My huff got lost amid Charlie's grunts of pain as he staggered to his feet.

"Sam doesn't . . . have the money, Bren."

"But the news reports? They all said she could claim the reward."

"She hasn't . . . squared that away . . . yet."

"Then I guess it's a good thing I threw everything I could in the car." Brenda hunched a shoulder under Charlie's armpit. "We'd better go hang out at Aunt Em's for a while."

"Wait a sec!" I protested. "You can't just disappear into the night. Tony's called the police. We have to report this assault."

"No, we don't."

"Yes, we do! I need a police report to put in a claim for the damage to my car."

I tried not to think of the hike in insurance rate I would get after a second claim in less than six months.

"You need medical attention, Charlie. And what about your truck?"

Teeth clenched against the pain, he eased into the passenger seat of Brenda's car. "Get the truck for me, will you, Sam? I'll . . ." He stopped, grunted, and started again. "I'll call the service department and let 'em know you'll pick it up."

"Oh, sure. Stick me for the repair bill, why don't you?"

"I'll pay you back."

"Uh-huh. Like you paid this Richie guy back?"

Since both he and Brenda had slammed their doors, the question was pretty much rhetorical. I stood there, thoroughly disgusted, while they drove off.

A black-and-white appeared about three minutes later. I provided what details I could. A medium-build guy I'd never seen before sprang out of the dark, went after my now-departed ex and me with a length of pipe, jumped in his car, and disappeared. Tony added that he was driving a light blue or gray, late-model Malibu with California plates.

When asked for the motive for the attack, I hesitated. Charlie was already in enough trouble. I hated to shovel more on him but saw no way out of sharing Brenda's frantic disclosures.

AFTER the drama of the day and evening, I had to force myself to sit down at my laptop and draft an email to my boss. I knew the fire incident would appear in DARPA's morning report. My only hope of salvation was to zing off a preliminary notification tonight, before he read the morning report.

I was stuck at "Hi, Dr. J" when my phone rang. Grabbing at the chance of even a temporary reprieve, I checked caller ID. I didn't recognize the number so I let it go to voice mail.

"Lieutenant Spade, this is DeWayne Wilson, Channel Nine News."

Oh, crap! I had a feeling I knew what was coming. Junior Reporter confirmed it with his next breathless disclosure.

"My producer just called. He picked up a report on the police scanner that an EPPD patrol officer responded to a nine-one-one call involving you tonight. He thought because of our, uh, past association you might fill me in on the details. Call me as soon as you can and . . ."

Sighing, I hit talk. "No comment."

"Lieutenant Spade? Is that you?"

"No."

I thoroughly enjoyed the ensuing five seconds of silence.

"It sounds like you," he said hesitantly.

I took pity on the guy. "All right. You caught me, DeWayne. But I can't comment on the incident tonight."

"Why not? Are you saying it's related to the Victor Duarte shooting?"

I started to dismiss the suggestion out of hand. Brenda had been so emphatic the attacker was after Charlie. When he'd ordered me to get in his car, I'd just assumed he'd mistaken me for Brenda and Richie the Mob Guy intended to force Charlie to pay up by kidnapping his wife.

Junior Reporter had now opened other, far more sinister, possibilities. Maybe someone had heard the story about the reward. Maybe they thought I'd already collected and decided to take a cut. What better way than to force me into a car and hold me for ransom? Or keep me incommunicado until the banks opened tomorrow morning and I could withdraw some cold, hard cash.

Or maybe, I thought as my stomach did a slow roll, whoever had hired Duarte was out for revenge.

"Gotta go," I mumbled.

I disconnected, feeling shell-shocked. How the heck had my life become so complicated? Longing for the days before severed heads and ex-husbands on the lam from the Mob, I decided Dr. J would have to wait. Right now I needed Ben and Jerry's Vanilla Caramel Fudge. And lots of it!

CHAPTER EIGHT

TWO heaping bowls of vanilla caramel fudge did the trick. Reenergized, I drafted a brief and shamelessly exculpatory email about the fire to Dr. J, fine-tuned it a couple of times, and zinged it off.

I hoped Mitch would call before I hit the sack, but I didn't hear from him. I was happy he and Jenny had these few precious days together but I was anxious to talk to him and bring him up to speed on the Charlie situation. I also wanted his take on Junior Reporter's suggestion there might be a connection between Pipe Guy and the Duarte shooting.

I figured that scary possibility would keep me tossing and turning all night, but I zonked right out. It did, however, make me exercise a bit more caution when I left for work the next morning.

My thumb hovered above the alarm button on my

keypad and I surveyed the parked cars carefully before I approached my own. In the bright light of day, the vicious dents and shattered taillights looked a whole lot nastier than they had last night. Sighing, I added three items to my already extensive mental checklist.

Take car in for estimate.

Get copy of police report.

Call insurance company.

Thank heavens I'm insured with USAA. The giant corporation is run by former military personnel and caters exclusively to active duty troops, retirees, honorably discharged veterans, and their dependents. Their fees are also graduated to fit military pay scales. As you might surmise, second lieutenants rank darn close to the bottom of the scale.

If I timed everything just right, I could drop my car off at the Chrysler dealership, hitch a ride to the Ford dealership, get Charlie's truck out of hock, and drive it until my car was repaired.

Or not.

If that *was* one of Richie Boy's goons last night and he *had* mistaken me for Brenda, it might not be too smart to tool around town in Charlie's pickup. For all Pipe Guy knew, his primary target was still in El Paso.

I decided to hold off on switching vehicles until I'd talked to my insurance company. So of course my defunct taillights got me stopped twice on my way to work. Once by an EPPD traffic cop and once by a Fort Bliss gate guard. Luckily, both bought my explanation of the recent nature of the damage and my promise to have it repaired as soon as possible.

I parked across the street again, but let myself in through the side door this time. Once inside, I recorded two immediate impressions. One, electrical power had been restored to our end of the hallway. The lights were on and the air-conditioning hummed quietly.

Two, my quivering nostrils picked up a powerful scent. Not the odor of damp or mold, although I fully expected both to set in after yesterday's fiasco. That was coffee I smelled, dark and rich and fresh.

I dumped my hat and purse on my desk and followed my nose to the break room. Before she'd left last night Pen had lined her tea canisters up like a row of Prussian soldiers. But one of the other team members had beat her in this morning, thank God, and brought a coffeemaker, microwave, and emergency supplies with him.

I had a good idea who. The industrial-size carton of PowerBars sitting beside the microwave pretty well IDed Noel. I filled a mug, snitched a peanut butter caramel crisp bar, and strolled down to his work area.

Here's the thing about noncoms. The good ones operate an intelligence network that makes the CIA look like an amateur enterprise. They're also world-class foragers. Especially Special Ops types like Noel. They get dropped behind enemy lines and can live off tree roots and grubs for months. In more civilized settings, nothing is safe around them unless it's nailed, soldered, or sutured. Even then I wouldn't turn my back on it.

Noel was on the phone. He waved a hand in greeting and finished his call while I polished off the PowerBar.

"Right. I'll be here. Thanks, Chief." He hung up with a satisfied grunt. "That was Sergeant Major Callahan at the Supply Depot. He's sending over temporary replacements for our computers. Should be here in a half hour."

"Great." I held up my mug. "Who donated the coffee-maker and microwave?"

"Sergeant Hawkins over at A Company. One of his artillery batteries just shipped out for a six-month rotation to Iraq. He let me, ah, borrow a few items."

Uh-oh. I'd met some of A Company's artillerymen. They didn't hear very well—the big guns do that to you—but you don't want to be on the receiving end of their multiple rocket launchers.

"We're not going to have those guys come looking for their stuff, are we?"

"Not to worry, Lieutenant. I'll make sure everything's back where it should be before they return."

"Who furnished the PowerBars?"

"Buddy Thompson at the gym. He ordered a dozen case lots for the Military Marathon a few months back. Some doofus in central purchasing screwed up and bought two dozen by mistake. Bud's been trying to get rid of 'em ever since."

His chair squeaking, Noel leaned back and looked around me.

"Charlie didn't come in with you? I told him I would take him to get his truck."

"You'll have to take me, instead. Charlie made an emergency exit last night."

"Huh?"

I heard arrival sounds and delayed an explanation. "I'll tell you about it at confab. We'd better grab a refill before Pen dumps the coffee and boils up some milk-weed and chrysanthemums or something."

Noel was already on his feet. We managed to snag fresh cups before a *tch-tch*ing Pen did her thing with the canisters and coffeemaker. When everyone had squeezed into my office for our morning session, I informed them that the perpetrator of yesterday's electrical blowout had flown the coop.

"Charlie had a couple of visitors last night. One came after us with a lead pipe. The other arrived a few moments later and . . ."

"Whoa! Back up a sec, Geardo Goddess!"

Dennis thumbed his glasses higher on the bridge of his nose. He was wearing all black today. Black high-tops, black jeans, black T-shirt displaying an ornate, medieval-style chess piece tipped on its side. Abstruse metaphors and symbols usually go right over my head but even I grasped that he was in mourning for his ruined Garry Kasparov poster.

"Someone attacked you and Charlie?" he echoed, bug-eyed. "With a pipe?"

When I nodded, Pen clucked her tongue in dismay. "You weren't hurt, were you?"

"I wasn't, but Charlie took a nasty hit. So did my Sebring," I added glumly.

I gave my team the details as I knew them. No one seemed particularly surprised to hear Charlie owed big bucks to the Mob. Or that he'd hoped that I would bail him out with a cut of the reward money.

The reason he'd gone into debt earned another tongue cluck from Pen and raised brows among the men.

Particularly when I told them Brenda Baby had descended on the scene all hyper and scared and carried Charlie off with her even before the cops arrived.

"They left you holding the bag?" Noel said.

"The bag and his truck."

"Huh. I kinda liked Charlie, but they shouldn't have skipped on you like that."

I chose not to remind him this wasn't the first time my ex and Brenda had done wrong by me. I was more interested in getting my team's opinion of Junior Reporter's post-incident speculation.

I was hoping they would collectively pooh-pooh the idea that I might have been the target of the attack, not Charlie. To my chagrin, the possibility produced an assortment of worried frowns and pursed lips.

"There could be a connection," Rocky said slowly. "Did the man who attacked you say anything?"

"Just 'get in the car.' I figured he mistook me for Brenda and planned to hold me as surety until Charlie came up with cash. It didn't occur to me to wonder if Pipe Guy could be connected to the Duarte mess until Cub Reporter DeWayne suggested it."

"Have you discussed this possibility with Mitch?"

"Not yet. He's out of town and we didn't connect last night."

"How about your friend at the FBI?"

"I guess I could call him," I said with a distinct lack of enthusiasm.

"Do it," Rocky urged with a nervous twitch. His thin shoulders hunched under his short-sleeved shirt. "You don't want to take unnecessary—"

He was interrupted by the jangle of my cell phone. I eyed the number on caller ID and groaned.

"Oh, Lord. It's Dr. J."

My team cleared out with the same speed they'd displayed the day a spotted skunk meandered through the open door of our D-FAC. Bracing my shoulders, I flipped up the phone.

I did my best to assure my boss that I had matters fully under control at this end. He almost choked on that one but eventually agreed the preliminary damage estimates weren't too heart-stopping. Still, he hung up with promises of dire retribution if I didn't submit the official reports on time and in proper format.

After that inauspicious start, my day went from crappy to god-awful. I made the requisite calls to EPPD to request a copy of the police report and to my insurance agent to alert her of a pending claim. She and I have come to know each other well in recent months. Not by choice on either side.

I then called the Chrysler service department to set up an appointment for a damage estimate. The service manager and I are on a first-name basis, too.

While I was talking to Hal, the deputy post commander's secretary beeped in with word that Colonel Roberts would like to see me in his office at fourteen hundred, if that was convenient. It was—mostly because I couldn't think of any way out of what I knew would be an uncomfortable session.

Rescheduling my missed JAG appointment was next

on my to-do list. The receptionist was a bit snippy about my no-show yesterday afternoon until I explained the reason for it. She then grudgingly agreed to slip me in.

"Can you come right now? Major Burke is with a client but should finish within the next ten or fifteen minutes."

"I'm on my way!"

THE Office of the Staff Judge Advocate occupies one of Fort Bliss's most historic buildings. Every time I drive past the 1890s-era two-story cavalry barracks, I can almost hear a bugler sounding assembly and the thunder of booted feet answering the call.

All I heard today was the sound of my own boots as I went up the front steps. Once inside, I consulted a directory with a bewildering array of information. For those of you who've never had to use the services of a JAG, they provide advice to both commanders and individual troops on civil and criminal matters. Their areas of expertise range from executing wills to paternity suits to claims for damages by civilians whose property was accidentally damaged by artillery fire to murder and mayhem.

When I'd called for the original appointment I wasn't sure where collecting a reward from a non-DOD agency might fall. Neither was the receptionist. After some consultation, she'd steered me to the Civil and Administrative Law Division. I'd subsequently checked the CALD out on the Fort Bliss website and knew it consisted of the chief, an NCOIC, two military attorneys, and three civilian attorneys.

My appointment was with a big, bluff, ruddy-faced major who looked like he might have played defensive tackle for West Point or Notre Dame. He was ushering out his previous client when I arrived, so I got ushered right in. Waving me to a seat in front of his desk, the major folded his impressive frame into a high-backed leather chair.

"I heard about you on the news, Lieutenant Spade. Nasty stuff, that business with the severed heads."

"Yes, sir."

"I also heard you helped take down the alleged killer."

"Me, and Staff Sergeant Noel Cassidy. That's what I wanted to talk to you about."

"Why?" Interest sparked in his blue eyes. "I know you can't believe even half of what you hear on the news, but it sounded like justifiable homicide to me. The civil authorities aren't trying to say otherwise, are they?"

"No."

Not according to my last conversation with Sheriff Alexander, anyway. I added a follow-up call to make sure to my mental checklist.

"The FBI had a substantial bounty out on the, ah, alleged killer. I don't know if Sergeant Cassidy and I can claim any of it, given the military's rules against accepting gifts or gratuities. I'm hoping you can tell me if rewards fall into that general category."

"Were the two of you on duty, conducting official business at the time?"

"We were."

"I'll have to research this further, but the only restriction I'm aware of pertains to the Rewards for Justice program. It offers monetary rewards for information leading to the capture and arrest of international terrorists."

"Like bin Laden," I said, nodding. "I read about that program."

"This guy you helped take down? He wasn't a terrorist, was he?"

"Just your common, garden-variety contract killer."

"Okay, let me check into this and get back to you."

"Thanks, Major." I had started to leave when a belated thought surfaced. "We were testing a device sent to us for evaluation by a civilian. The device was what led to the discovery of the heads and subsequent shooting, so there may be proprietary issues involved, too."

"That could certainly complicate matters." His mouth curved. "You don't do anything by half, do you, Lieutenant?"

"Not if I can help it."

I left the JAG offices and decided I needed a decent lunch to fortify myself for my afternoon session with the deputy post commander. A quick call to my troops had them saddling up to meet at the Applebee's not far from the base. I have a fatal weakness for the restaurant's Triple Chocolate Meltdown, but consuming one is a team sport.

Despite my preparatory measures, my meeting with Colonel Roberts did not go well. An artilleryman born and bred, he used his office to showcase his collection of spent shells from every weapon in the Army's arsenal. Nothing like a display of 155mm shell casings to intimidate all comers.

Not that Colonel "Iron Butt" Roberts needed additional props. He was thin to the point of desiccation and lacked anything remotely resembling a sense of humor. He began our session by reminding me of the fire out at our test site last year—as if I could forget it!—and wanted to know why FST-3 hadn't taken the necessary precautions to preclude a recurrence.

"Respectfully, sir, the previous fire was caused by an arsonist. This one was caused by . . ."

"Your ex-husband," he snapped.

"I was going to say faulty wiring."

He brushed that aside. "Mind telling me what a civilian was doing on post, in your office, playing with an experimental device?"

I stuck to the truth, such as it was. "He was in El Paso on business, sir. I brought him on post to show him where I work."

As you might surmise, my response didn't particularly sit well with the colonel. It didn't sit well me, either, but was the best I could do. I said another fervent prayer of thanksgiving that I'd followed proper procedures and checked Charlie in before Iron Butt delivered a stiff warning that he would personally review the reports of damage to determine culpability.

"Yes, sir."

"That's all, Lieutenant."

Any junior officer with half a thought to making a

career of the military would have beat a strategic retreat at that point. Since my future in the military was iffy at best, I figured I had nothing to lose.

"Actually, sir, I've been wanting to talk to you about the renovations I've requested for our building."

"Lieutenant . . ."

I ignored the warning growl.

"The engineers worked a temporary fix to the electrical wiring, but they said they'll have to reassess the entire system."

Thunderclouds gathered in the colonel's eyes.

"The electrical wiring in that building is up to code, Lieutenant Spade. I wouldn't allow you or anyone else to work there if it wasn't."

"Yes, sir. I mean, no, sir. But the HVAC system sucks and the fort's original occupants must have carted the toilets out here with them in covered wagons. As long as the engineers are working in the building, you could have them take a look at the plumbing and air-conditioning, too."

The colonel's chair scraped the floor. His fists balled on his desk. If looks were 155mm howitzer shells, I'd have a hole the size of the Chunnel bored through my midsection right now.

"For the last time, Lieutenant, the improvements you've requested are under review by our Facilities Management Board. They'll evaluate your submissions and, if approved, prioritize them against all other requirements to be effected *if* and *when* funding becomes available."

"Yes, but . . ."

"You Are Dismissed."

Most folks, my mother included, will tell you I'm somewhat lacking in the self-preservation gene. Yet even I take heed when someone speaks to me in Capital Letters.

I saluted, executed a semi-respectable about face, and got the hell out of Dodge.

THE only saving grace to my whole crappy day was the phone call from Mitch later that night. To my relief, he'd smoothed things over between Jenny and her mom and planned to fly home tomorrow evening.

"I get in at six fifteen."

"Great. I'll pick you up at the airport. We can have dinner."

"Then we'll finish what we started Saturday morning."

The husky promise raised instant goose bumps on my arms. Banishing all thoughts of Charlie, Pipe Guy, and Colonel Iron Butt, I headed for the bathroom to shave my legs.

CHAPTER NINE

WHAT'S that old saying? Every dog has its day?

Mine was Wednesday.

Everything went right for a change. Not only did I complete the damage report a whole four days before it was due, I begged, bribed, and cajoled the technicians checking the building's electrical system into taking a look at the power supply for the heating and air-conditioning system. They insisted there was sufficient power going to the units but agreed the units themselves were inadequate to cool the cubic airspace in our building. I even got them to put that in writing!

Then, just before noon, Major Burke called to inform me that he didn't see any legal or ethical impediment to Sergeant Cassidy or I accepting a reward offered by the FBI as long as it wasn't part of the Rewards for Justice program.

I whooped and started hearing cash registers ping again. The major added a caveat in mid-ping.

"I researched Army, Air Force, and DOD regs. There may be something in DARPA's internal operating procedures, though, particularly as concerns the proprietary properties of the device you were testing. I strongly suggest you run this by DARPA's legal experts."

"I will. Thanks! And if it's not a conflict of interest or blatant fraternization between the ranks, I'll buy you a steak dinner if and when the FBI comes through with the reward."

Laughing, he accepted the offer. "You're on, Lieutenant."

I whooped again and did a happy dance down the hall. Heads popped out along my route and I soon had the senior members of FST-3 dogging my heels to Sergeant Cassidy's cubicle.

"Noel! I just heard from the major."

A wary expression instantly dropped over his face. "My shrink called you." He braced his shoulders. "She said she would have to. Professional ethics and all that."

"Huh?"

"I swear, Lieutenant, spending the night at her place was her idea, not mine."

I won't say my jaw hit the floor, but it came damned close. On reflection, I guess I shouldn't have been surprised. The last time Major Honeycutt had provided me a prognosis for Noel's return to his unit, she'd smiled and said she didn't see it happening any time in the near future.

"No," I got out eventually, "I haven't heard from your shrink. I was talking about the major at the JAG office. He says he doesn't see any reason why we can't collect the reward. He said we should run it by DARPA's legal beagles just to be sure, but it's looking good at this point. Very good! Assuming," I added on an afterthought, "Pancho thinks we deserve a cut."

I hadn't talked to Pancho since I'd first heard about the reward. For all I knew, Lawyer Nowatny had approached him, too, and convinced him to claim the entire amount.

I wouldn't argue if he did. Despite the visions of designer shoes dancing through my head, I refused to sink to the kind of ugly squabbles so endemic in my family. Like the one my mother and her sister got into over which of their offspring should inherit my bachelor uncle Pete's '67 Dodge Dart. Didn't matter that none of us wanted it! The thing was a heap of peeling paint held together by rust and sitting on cinder blocks. Bottom line? Mom and Aunt Grace haven't spoken to each other in a decade. Determined to tread cautiously on the potentially touchy matter of the reward, I hit speed dial.

Pancho answered on the fourth ring. *"Hola."*

"It's me, Panch."

"Hi, Sam. How you doing?"

"Good. Mostly. You haven't had a visit from someone who wanted to put a dent in your skull, have you?"

"No," he answered warily. "Have you?"

"Maybe."

That led to a long and somewhat disjointed explanation of my ex's unexpected reappearance in my life, his financial troubles, his hope that I would fork over big bucks from the reward, and an attack by someone who might—or might not—have been acting as a collector for the Mob. At that point I shared Junior Reporter's speculation that the creep who hired Duarte might have been behind the attack.

Pancho listened in silence through all this. When I finished, I could almost hear the careless shrug in his response.

"Anyone wants to come after me for taking down a stone-cold killer, they're welcome to try. Is Pen there?"

"What?"

"Pen. Is she there?"

"Yes, but . . ."

"Let me talk to her. I have to tell her I tried the alfalfa mint blend she recommended. She was right, Sam. It loosened me up like you wouldn't believe."

Loosened him up how, I didn't want to know.

"I'll put her on in a minute. First, I need to talk to you about the reward."

"What about it?"

"Well . . . The thing is . . ."

This was more awkward than I'd anticipated. How do you ask someone if he minds pocketing thirty-three thousand instead of a whole hundred grand?

"I talked to a military JAG yesterday about whether Noel and I can accept part of the FBI reward. He says we can, but first I need to make sure you don't object to us claiming a share of . . ."

"You can have it all."

"What?"

"I've seen what blood money can do to a man. I don't want any of it."

"But . . ."

"Not interested, Lootenant."

"Are you sure? We're talking major dollars here."

More than enough to patch the cracks in the adobe and update the decor in his smoke-blackened bar/restaurant/etc.

"I'm sure. Now can I talk to Pen?"

Wordlessly, I handed over the phone. While Pen turned away, cradling the phone to her ear, I relayed Pancho's decision to the rest of the group.

"He doesn't want the reward."

Dennis's brows shot up. Rocky blinked and fiddled with the pens in his plastic pocket holder. Noel looked confused.

"Why not?"

"He says it's blood money. He doesn't want any part of it."

Blood money or not, I have to confess that I heard those cash registers again. Much louder this time.

Hey! Don't go all righteous and judgmental. I'm no more avaricious than the next gal. How would you react if someone handed you an extra seventeen grand?

"Pancho may change his mind," I cautioned Noel. "That would be okay with me."

"Me, too."

"However it works out, we'll probably both be able to pay our bills with change to spare. What do you say we celebrate by taking our fellow team members out to eat?"

"Lunch, or dinner?"

"Lunch," I said firmly. "Mitch's plane gets in at six fifteen. I have plans for dinner."

And dessert.

NOEL and I let the others choose where they wanted to go for lunch. Dennis suggested his favorite all-you-can-eat buffet. Pen, naturally, opted for a natural foods deli, but Rocky really wanted to try a sushi bar that just opened outside the west gate. Since it would likely close within a month—West Texans aren't particularly partial to raw fish—we yielded to his choice.

I'm not real partial to raw fish, either, but I thoroughly enjoyed chowing down with my team. The restaurant was almost empty, so we got great service and the chef offered to whip up special delicacies that weren't on the menu. Noel and Dennis jumped at the offer and requested anything cooked. They regretted their choice when the beaming chef presented a whole Chilean sea bass, complete with beady eyes and needle sharp teeth, decked out on a bed of spinach and rice.

Since it was a duty day we substituted ginger tea for ginger beer, which earned smiles of approval from Pen but made getting the sushi down more of an effort. Despite the challenge, I consumed my share.

I'd asked Noel to ride with me so we could swing by the Ford dealership on the way back. Surprise, surprise! Charlie had actually remembered to call and tell them I would be picking up his truck. Two hundred and twenty-six dollars later, I followed Noel to his apartment. We left the truck there and drove back to work.

I did my best to keep busy until we quit for the day. I usually head home around five or five thirty but left a little early to primp prior to picking Mitch up.

Imagine my dismay when, in the midst of my preparations, I discovered I'd developed a serious case of fish breath. I brushed my teeth, gargled, brushed again, and popped wintergreen-flavored Tic Tacs all the way to the airport.

Mitch called when his plane touched down, so I was waiting at the curb when he walked out of the terminal. He looked so damned good with his long, easy stride and the sun burnishing his dark gold hair, that my toes curled against the soles of my flip-flops.

I'd worn my dressiest pair in Mitch's honor. He calls them my Dorothy flops because of their two-inch-thick ruby red soles and sequined straps. I'd teamed them with snug jeans and a similarly sequined red tank. The color brought out the auburn highlights in my hair, which I'd left down—also in Mitch's honor, although I'd had to tie it back during the drive to keep it from slashing my face and putting out an eye.

I had it properly tamed when Mitch tossed his carry-all in the back and slid into the passenger seat. I leaned across the console and into his kiss, hoping the Tic Tacs had performed as advertised.

Evidently so, as he tugged me back for a second round before stretching out his legs and laying his arm across the back of my seat. "What's with the dents and busted taillights? Or should I ask?"

Mitch and I had met during my pre-Sebring days, when I drove a Bronco with more scratches than paint.

He's ridden with me often enough since to know how the scratches got there.

"Long story," I said, ignoring the way his foot instinctively stomped the floorboard as I muscled my way into airport traffic. "First tell me how it went with Jenny."

"A lot tougher than I'd expected. She's changed so much since I last saw her."

"Two years is a pretty big leap in a girl's life," I agreed. "She's about at the age where we stop playing with dolls and start playing with boys."

"That's the real bone of contention between Jen and her mother," he said wryly. "Her so-called boyfriend. I gotta tell you, Samantha, it was hard as hell to remain neutral on that one. The jerk decks himself out in what Jen informed me is the emo look."

"Dyed hair with a long sweep across his forehead, facial piercings, lots of eyeliner, band T-shirts, and black, skinny-leg jeans?"

"You nailed it. He's not a bad kid as far as I could tell, but he's got so many holes in his head I swear his brains have leaked out. He's as thick as a board about everything but music."

"You didn't share that opinion with Jenny, did you?"

"I refrained but damned near bit my tongue off in the process."

Lord, I hoped not! I knew from personal experience what he could do with that tongue.

We spent the rest of the drive to his place discussing his efforts to get to know the woman his daughter was fast becoming.

* * *

MITCH lives in an older neighborhood of ranch-style homes with swing sets and plastic Big Wheels dotting the yards. He insisted Margo take whatever she wanted when she and Jenny moved out. The woman literally cleaned house.

When we started seeing each other the place contained only the bare essentials. Since then Mitch has added some little luxuries—like a chenille bathmat so I don't have to step out of the shower onto cold tile and the oversized, buttery soft leather sofa that sits three and sleeps two with room to spare. I had the sofa in mind as our eventual destination when we came in through the kitchen. Mitch had other ideas. Dropping his carryall, he caught my elbow and swung me around.

"God, I missed you!"

"I missed you, too."

"I'd forgotten how bad it was with Margo. The tension. The resentment. The anger always simmering just below the surface." He tunneled his fingers through my hair and tipped my face to his. "You've made me forget, Samantha."

My heart pumped. That was as close as we'd come to the L word. I was about to make the final leap when he bent his head and trapped the words in my throat.

I've been kissed by a fair number of men. Yet I've never tasted the kind of slow, sweet hunger Mitch rouses in me. Or felt my entire body tighten in response the mere touch of his mouth on mine.

We didn't make it to the sofa. Not the first time, anyway. Slow and sweet turned hot and heavy in a hurry. I won't say it was my first time making love on a kitchen table, but it sure as heck was the most intensely, incredibly erotic. Mitch used his teeth and tongue and hands to ignite sparks in parts of me I didn't know were combustible. I did my best to return the favor but he soon had me groaning and locking my calves around his hips.

IT wasn't until later, much later, that he asked me about Charlie. We'd adjourned to the bedroom by then. I was so depleted from our reunion that it took me a moment to dredge the details from my near-comatose brain.

"Charlie took off with Brenda."

"Who?"

"The top-heavy bimbette he borrowed all that money for."

"Oh. Right. His wife. She followed him to El Paso?"

"She wasn't the only one."

Drawing on my last reserves of energy, I rolled my boneless body over enough to prop an arm on his chest. While he played with the ends of my hair I told him about: (1) Charlie sparking an electrical fire; (2) Pipe Guy's attack; (3) Brenda's sudden arrival; (4) her abrupt departure with Snoogs; and (5) the nasty possibilities raised by Junior Reporter.

As expected, the idea the attack might have been directed against me and not Charlie preempted everything else in Mitch's mind.

"Hell, Samantha." He gave my hair a swift tug. "Why didn't you call and tell me about all this?"

"You were busy with Jenny. Besides, there was nothing you could do."

"I could have called Paul Donati. Had him set up some surveillance at your place." He gave my hair another tug. "Or *you* could have called him."

I wasn't about to admit I'd been more preoccupied with the fire and the question of the reward.

"I'll call him tomorrow," I promised.

"Damn straight, you will. Until then, I'm not letting you out of my sight."

MITCH held true to his word.

He insisted I stay with him that night and followed me home early the next morning. A rosy dawn was lighting up the sky when I unlocked the door to my apartment. Mitch checked the interior, fished my cell phone out of my purse, and handed it over with a brusque order.

"Call Donati."

"It's too early. He won't be in yet."

"They have a duty officer on call twenty-four/seven. Tell him or her it's a code nine and they'll patch you through."

"What's a code nine?"

"You don't need to know. Just make the call."

I popped him a salute. "Yes, sir!"

"Now, Samantha."

"All right, already."

"And let me talk to Paul when you're through."

I think I mentioned how cops tend to close ranks. Border Patrol agents are no exception. After the FBI duty officer got Donati on the line and I went through the litany again, Mitch gestured impatiently for me to hand him the phone.

"Get a copy of the responding EPPD officer's report, Paul. Have them fax me a copy, too. Maybe we'll pick up on something they missed. In the meantime, I want Samantha covered."

He listened for several moments, cutting me a wry glance.

"Yeah. Yeah. I know! But she didn't instigate this attack. Okay, not directly. But you can't lay Duarte and those severed heads on her."

"He'd better not!" I said indignantly.

"Just set up some electronic surveillance. I'll keep her on a short leash until it's in place."

Leash? Did he just say leash?

My feathers puffed up like those of a western sage grouse in full attack mode. If you've never seen one, they're pretty scary. I know because I'd flushed a hen from her nest by accident some months back and had to fend off her highly irate mate.

Isn't it amazing what a difference a phone call can make? Less than twelve hours ago I'd been a kiss away from telling this man I loved him. Now I was all indignant and within a breath of suggesting he take his collapsible baton and . . .

Mitch snapped the phone shut before I completed the thought. "Paul says he'll have a team here in an hour."

CHAPTER TEN

DONATI'S team arrived at my door in less than fifty minutes. Unfortunately, Special Agent Donati arrived with them.

I don't know all that many FBI agents so I don't have a good database to compare Paul to. But I suspect not all field agents are as intimidating as he is. Given his dark, bedroom eyes and curly black hair, I'm not sure how he manages to project such a one-false-move-and-you're-dead aura. He does, though. Trust me on this. He's projected it more than once in my direction.

While his team went to work, Paul explained his quick response to my call. "DEA got a lead on the scuzz who hired Duarte to take out those three drug dealers up in Wisconsin. Word is he's out to take over the entire Midwest market."

It still gave me a twinge to think the drug barons of

Central America and Mexico had extended their territory so far north. When I said as much to Paul, he burst my bubble.

"This baron is homegrown. He was born in a suburb of St. Louis called Dutchtown, hence his nickname Dutch, or the Dutchman. Bastard moved with his parents to L.A. when he was in his early teens and joined a gang. Didn't take him long to graduate to the big time. Drugs, prostitution, racketeering—you name it, Dutch stuck a hand in every pot. Moved up the ladder by eliminating competitors and exacting swift, brutal revenge against anyone who crossed him. Or interfered with his operation."

"Uh-oh."

" 'Uh-oh' doesn't begin to describe this guy. We've been trying to nail him for five years, but he's slick as spit. He's also as ruthless as they come."

Not what I wanted to hear.

"I wish we had hard evidence that it was one of the Dutchman's goons who attacked you. If so, we could use the attack to get to the man himself."

I didn't particularly want to hear that, either.

"My ex thought Pipe Guy was a Mob enforcer," I said, clutching at any straw, "sent to collect on the fifteen grand Charlie owes some guy named Richie."

"That's possible," Donati conceded. "I've got the folks in our Vegas office checking it out."

"Or it could have been someone who heard about the reward and wanted a cut."

"Also possible. And good reason to give you some security."

"What about Sergeant Cassidy?" I asked with an eye to the two technicians mounting a camera in the corner of my living room. "And Pancho. Don't they need surveillance, too?"

"Pancho refused it. We don't think Sergeant Cassidy's at risk since he was never mentioned by name in any of the news reports. You were the one whose name and face got splashed all over the airwaves."

I made a silent vow to cut Cub Reporter DeWayne off at the knees the next time our paths crossed. I added Special Agent Donati to my personal hit list when he couldn't resist a dig at my expense.

"You might want to think about lowering your profile, Lieutenant. Or better yet, refrain from getting stabbed, shot at, or run off the road."

Mitch came to my defense while I was still sputtering with indignation. "Give her a break, Paul. Samantha doesn't go looking for trouble."

"She doesn't have to," Donati drawled. "It sniffs her out. Like that crazy device she was testing when she locked horns with Duarte."

I went still, but my mind shot off into the ionosphere. Good grief! Was it possible . . . ?

"You don't suppose . . . ?" I stopped, shook my head. "No, that's too far out."

"What is?" Paul asked.

"The device we were testing. I don't know if you saw all the negative publicity . . ."

"That stuff about feeding off corpses and desecrating war dead? I saw it."

"Snoop doesn't feed just on dead things."

"Snoop?" His brows lifting, Paul turned to Mitch. "You want to ask?"

"We probably shouldn't but what the hell. 'Snoop,' Samantha?"

"As in Snoopy Sniffer. The children's toy."

I could tell by their blank expressions they'd never owned one or bought one for their kids. If Paul had kids. I'd have to ask. Later.

"The device's inventor labeled it a Self-Nurturing Find and Identify Robot," I explained. "SNFIR for short. So my team dubbed it Snoopy . . ."

"Sniffer," Mitch finished. "We get it. What's your point?"

"My point is that Snoop has the potential to become a perpetual motion machine. Suppose someone like the Dutchman saw one of those sensational TV stories or Internet blogs? Suppose he got to thinking about a new delivery vehicle for his products? One that could scoot across vast stretches of desert, avoid checkpoints and patrols, and arrive at a specific location, at a specified time."

I had their full attention now. Also that of the two technicians. One hung on his ladder, wires sprouting from both hands. The other had a boot planted on the bottom rung and his fascinated gaze locked on me.

"That's one scenario we haven't considered," Paul admitted after a lengthy pause. "Where's this device now?"

"In my office."

"The office your ex-husband set on fire?"

I didn't remember telling Donati about the fire, but at this point the days and the players were all starting to blur.

"Charlie didn't spark much more than an electrical outage. And Snoopy didn't sustain any damage."

"Good." He extracted a BlackBerry from his shirt pocket and paged down to his calendar. "How about I come out to Fort Bliss around ten thirty this morning and you show me how Snoopy works?"

"Not a problem. Do you want a demonstration, too, Mitch?"

"I do, but it'll have to be some other time. I promised my boss I'd take patrol this morning." He checked his watch. "I'd better hit the road. Before I leave, Paul, tell me how you'll track Samantha."

Donati waved a hand, deferring to the technical specialist with a fistful of wires.

"We've installed motion detectors here in the apartment," the agent on the ladder informed both Mitch and me. "Also high-def video cameras with wireless transmitters. The parking area's covered, too."

"What about when she's in transit?"

The tech climbed off the ladder and dug a small, flat object out of his bag of tricks.

"This sucker will pick up signals from Mars. All you have to do is keep it on your person, Lieutenant. We'll track you street by street, block by block."

He passed me the device, which was almost identical to the keypad for the Sebring's door locks.

When I said as much to the tech, he nodded. "That's the idea. Put it on your key ring so you have it with you wherever you go. If you're in distress, just press this red button. It'll set off a silent alarm that . . . No! Wait, Lieutenant!"

Too late. My thumb had already squished the button.

Muttering under his breath, the tech snatched a radio from his belt. "Comm, this is Strahan. Ignore distress signals emanating from tracking device Charlie Foxtrot Seven-Four-Four-Nine."

"Charlie Foxtrot?"

I threw Donati an accusing glare. His smirk told he knew damned well those initials from the NATO phonetic alphabet conveyed several succinct messages, only one of which was politically correct.

"The alarm connects to our central control," the tech informed me after his contact had reset the device. "We can relay the signal instantly to other local and regional law enforcement agencies and effect a response within minutes, much as we do for an AMBER Alert."

I tried to convince myself an electronic leash made sense, especially with Mob bosses and/or Dutchmen out for my blood. Felt kind of odd being hooked into a system designed for kidnapped children, though.

"The Border Patrol's plugged into the alert system, too," Mitch advised. "I'll make sure the people on our desk keep an eye on you."

He checked his watch again.

"I've got to go. Call me when you leave work. I'll bring a few things over and camp out here at your place till this is over. If that's good with you?"

My toes did the curl thing again. "Very good."

"I'll see you after work, then. And for God's sake, don't try to be a hero. If anything looks or feels or sounds the least bit suspicious, press the panic button."

"Don't worry, I will."

* * *

AND I would have. I swear!

The problem was that the FBI in all their brilliance made their handy-dandy panic device look *too* much like an ordinary keypad.

I discovered that when Paul Donati and the two technicians walked me to my car. By then I'd made a quick change into my uniform, clipped up my hair, slapped on some lip gloss, slung my purse over my shoulder, and grabbed my soft-sided briefcase. I kept my car keys in hand as I approached the Sebring but had to look twice to figure out which keypad popped the locks.

"Yours is square," Paul pointed out with exaggerated patience. "Ours is oblong."

I was tempted to respond with another string of letters from the NATO phonetic alphabet. Something along the lines of Bravo Foxtrot Delta. That's BFD in non-NATO-ese. Nobly, I refrained.

Paul and company followed me until I exited I-10 for Patriot Freeway and the short stretch leading to Fort Bliss's main entrance. With the post in sight, I decided it would be safe to make a quick stop at the donut shop in the strip mall just outside the gate.

I hit the place between waves of sweet-toothed military and civil service employees. Without the usual long line, I got in and out in mere minutes with a coffee to go and an assorted dozen. Included among the French crullers and cranberry muffins were three of Rocky's favorite lemon-filled. I'm not ashamed to admit I intended them as a bribe. I hoped they would silence any possible objections to firing up Snoopy's computers for an unscheduled, unofficial test.

True, this test had been requested by another government agency. Rocky and I had both taken some hits in the past on just this subject, however. The darts bounced off me but Dr. Balboa tends to internalize criticism. Actually, he internalizes everything and gets his feelings hurt in the process.

Rumor is he expressed those feelings very forcefully on at least one occasion, which resulted in his assignment to FST-3. I haven't been able to substantiate the rumor, but I was thinking about a certain eyebrow-less scientist I'd bumped into at DARPA headquarters some months ago as I walked to my car.

I was halfway there when my cell phone sounded Mitch's ring tone. I juggled coffee, donuts, and car keys to dig in my uniform pocket.

"You on base yet?" he wanted to know.

"Almost. I can see the front gate."

"Don't forget to call me when you leave work."

"I won't."

"Good enough. I'll see you . . ."

"I know," I cut in with a smile. "When you see me."

I was still smiling when a smoke black SUV with darkened windows cut across the parking lot and pulled up beside me. One glance at the driver sent my heart into my throat.

"Oh, hell!"

Pipe Guy was at the wheel. Someone wearing aviator glasses occupied the passenger seat. I tossed the coffee and donut box and fumbled frantically with my key ring, but Pipe Guy's pal leaped out just as I stabbed the red button. The wrong red button, dammit. The Sebring's horn started honking at the same instant Aviator Glasses reached over and stabbed *me*.

The needle was thin and sharp enough to pierce my supposedly heat-and-cold-resistant ABUs. I barely felt the pinprick, but whatever the bastard pumped into me worked fast. I managed one screech that even I couldn't hear over the honking horn before my throat started to close.

My lips went numb. The keys slipped from my suddenly nerveless fingers. My knees buckled.

My last hope—my only hope!—was that the Sebring's alarm had alerted folks inside the donut place. I couldn't tell if it had. The SUV blocked my view of the shop windows.

A second later I couldn't see anything at all.

I woke with the world's worst case of cotton mouth.

My tongue felt ten times its normal size. My throat was bone dry. My salivary glands had gone on strike. My eyelids weren't functioning properly, either, as I discovered when I tried to pry them open.

Nothing wrong with my hearing, however. A roar pierced the fog in my head. It was so loud and steady my confused brain soon identified it. That was an engine bouncing sound waves off my eardrums.

Correction. Two engines. I verified that when I finally forced my lids up over eyeballs that felt as pitted and rough as an unpaved road.

At that point I discovered I was flat on my back. In a small, prop aircraft. Minus the usual amenities like rear compartment seats. This one had been stripped and was obviously used primarily to haul cargo. I surmised as much from the tie-down straps dangling from the fuselage struts and the ringbolts welded to the flooring—one of which I was handcuffed to.

Frowning, I tugged on the cuff. The resulting rattle brought the two occupants of the open cockpit slewing around in their seats.

"About time you woke up," a guy with mirrored sunglasses shouted over the engine's whine. "We're about to begin our descent."

I recognized Pipe Guy's pal behind the dark glasses. That wasn't Pipe Guy in the pilot's seat, though.

Swallowing in a desperate attempt to kick-start my salivary glands, I unstuck my tongue and forced out a hoarse croak. "Descent to where? Hey! You with the glasses! Where are we landing?"

He either didn't hear or chose to ignore me. My money was on the latter. I swallowed once more and tried to clear the last fingers of the fog.

A weapon. I needed a weapon.

The cuffs rattled as I scooted around on the corrugated decking. My dry throat closed again when I spotted a toolbox strapped down at the rear of the cargo compartment.

I shot a quick glance forward, saw the two men in the cockpit were otherwise engaged, and slithered across the deck like a python in tiger stripes.

Steel bit through the skin of my wrist. My elbow and shoulder joints screamed in protest. The toe of my boot angled toward the latch of the strap securing the toolbox. I couldn't reach it.

I strained harder, biting my lip until I tasted blood, but couldn't stretch that final inch. Even if I had, I wouldn't have had time to get the box open before the aircraft banked sharply and began a steep descent.

Frustrated and aching and starting to get scared, I pushed into a sitting position. I was braced against the fuselage when we touched down. We taxied only a short distance before the pilot cut the engines.

Aviator Glasses unlatched his seat harness and came back to the rear compartment. Hunkering down, he slid his glasses to the tip of his nose and let his eyes drift from my bit lip to my bloody wrist. When they lifted and met mine, that wasn't sympathy I saw in them.

"I'm going to unlock the cuff. Don't try anything stupid, Lieutenant. I'll put you out again at the first sign of trouble. Understood?"

I wanted to flip him the finger but settled for nodding.

"Just out of curiosity," I rasped through my still-dry throat, "what did you inject me with?"

"The same paralyzing agent used in hospitals and ERs to relax muscles and put patients out before they insert breathing tubes and stuff. Not a problem unless you're allergic to it."

"How . . . ?" I had to stop and lick my lips again. "How did you know I wasn't?"

"I didn't."

The response chilled me almost as much as his careless shrug. It also told me the odds were pretty high that I wouldn't leave wherever I was alive.

I tried to shake off the terror that thought generated as Sunglasses released the cuff attached to the ringbolt. Yanking my arm forward, he snapped the cuff on my other wrist, then hooked a hand under my armpit and hauled me to my feet.

"Let's go."

"Go where?" I rasped as he shoved me toward the steps the pilot had let down.

"You'll know soon enough."

I stumbled down the steps into sunshine so dazzling I had to squeeze my eyes against the glare. It gradually reduced enough for me to spot a Hummer waiting with the engine idling . . . and what looked like a sheer, thousand-foot drop beyond it.

I staggered back, glancing wildly from right to left. My stunned mind took several seconds to grasp the fact that we'd touched down atop a massive plateau jutting out of the empty desert. Pen would object to that characterization, I thought, gulping back a bubble of near hysteria. As she reminds us ad nauseam, the desert is anything but empty.

This one showed no signs of human habitation, though. No baked adobe-brick farmhouse. No fence lines. No slowly twisting windmill pumping precious water into tin cattle troughs.

Where the hell was I? New Mexico? Arizona? Somewhere south of the border? Nothing in the austerely magnificent landscape gave me a clue. The driver of the

Hummer, the two pilots, and I could have been alone in the universe.

My eerie sense of isolation lasted only until Aviator Glasses manhandled me into the backseat of the Hummer and climbed in beside me. The driver gave me a curious glance in the rearview mirror, but I didn't see anything remotely resembling sympathy in his dark eyes as he put the heavy wheeler in gear and pulled away from the dirt airstrip. Only after we'd bumped and humped for a good half mile across the top of the mesa did I see the walled compound.

It was flat-roofed and two-tiered, with the ends of massive lodgepole pines butting through the walls at regular intervals. The construction reminded me of pictures I'd seen of the ancient Anasazi pueblos. But the security cameras and sensors that monitored our approach were ultra high-tech and *very* twenty-first century. So was the Uzi cradled in the arm of the guard who waved us through a wrought-iron gate.

Who owned this high desert dwelling? I ran through all the possibilities, from Charlie's nemesis Richie to some greedy bastard wanting in on the reward to the slime who'd hired Duarte and now wanted revenge.

None of those possibilities, however, came anywhere close to the bone-chilling reality.

CHAPTER ELEVEN

THE Hummer passed through a wooden gate and pulled up under a low portico. When Aviator Glasses hustled me out of the vehicle, I picked up the steady hum off to the side of the main building. Generators, I guessed. Anyone who lived on the top of an isolated mesa like this had to supply his own water and power.

"Inside."

Sunglasses gave me an impatient shove. I stumbled over a raised threshold into a two-story foyer dominated by a larger-than-life-sized metal sculpture of an eagle dancer. If my wrists hadn't been handcuffed and my stomach twisted in knots, I might have appreciated the scupltor's incredible artistry. I didn't give the piece a second glance, however. My entire being was focused on the woman who emerged from the cool, dim interior.

The slender brunette clicked toward us on red stilettos

with four-inch heels and a black powder puff on each ankle strap. My first, completely irrelevant thought was that the slut shoes didn't go with her slim skirt, belted white blouse, and the half glasses perched on the end of her nose. Those gave her an almost professional look . . . and made me feel like a total grunge by comparison. I resisted the ridiculous urge to raise my cuffed hands and brush back the hair hanging in rattails around my face. I straightened my shoulders, though, and lifted my chin.

It shot up another notch when the brunette treated me to a look of utter disdain before firing a stream of Spanish at my escort. I've picked up a basic working vocabulary during my assignment to El Paso but her dialogue came too fast. All I caught were "this one" and "*el patron*" and "tonight."

Whatever she said put Aviator Glasses on the defensive. He fired back but Slut Shoes cut him off with a rapier look and terse order.

"Espera aqui!"

That I got. She wanted us to wait there in the foyer. Whoever this bitch was, she wielded considerable power. The knowledge didn't give me a warm fuzzy.

But when the woman returned some moments later, her attitude had done a one-eighty. Subdued and almost obsequious, she trailed a half step behind a tall, dark-haired male in pleated white slacks and a blue and gold Versace shirt. I recognized the designer—I should, given the variety of glamour mags I subscribe to—but not the wearer. Deciding offense was the best defense, I looked him square in the eye.

"You're aware kidnapping a United States Air Force officer is a federal offense, aren't you?"

"Kidnapping is a federal offense regardless of race, creed, religion, or military affiliation," he replied in perfect and clearly amused English. "In your country, that is. In mine, it's more of a political necessity."

I don't like being laughed at any more than I like being injected, cuffed, and manhandled.

"You think this is funny? You'd better enjoy it while you can."

"I will. I most certainly will."

His reply conveyed such silky menace that even Slut Shoes blinked. It made an impression on me, too, but I refused to let him see it. Chin angled, I telegraphed an unmistakable up-yours.

The message missed its mark since Versace had already turned to my escort. "You may remove the lieutenant's cuffs."

"Are you sure, *patron*?"

"I'm sure. Even if she manages to get past security and escape, she has nowhere to go but into the desert. She would not get far in this heat."

Aviator Glasses complied but kept a wary eye on me as his boss addressed the brunette.

"Teresa, please show Lieutenant Spade to the room we're prepared for her. I'm sure she would like to refresh herself and change into something more comfortable before lunch."

I already knew this was no ordinary snatch-and-grab. Still, the idea these characters had anticipated my arrival made my stomach cramp.

"What the lieutenant would like," I said, rubbing my bruised and lacerated wrists, "is to know what the hell is going on."

"I'll explain at lunch."

Obviously used to being obeyed, he turned to leave. That pissed me off almost as much as his amusement.

"Hey! You!"

Aviator Glasses let out a hiss. Slut Shoes sucked one in. Versace turned slowly. Very slowly. His eyes showed dead black above the blue and gold of his shirt.

"I'll allow you that one, Lieutenant. But only that one. For the rest of our association, you will address me with respect."

Okay, now I was officially intimidated. This guy was scary. Don't ask me where I got the guts—or the stupidity—to force my lips into a sugary smile.

"Kind of hard to address you at all when I don't know your name."

"Mendoza. Rafael Mendoza."

Shock knocked the smart-mouthiness out of me. I stood there, my breath stuck like a broken glass in my throat, and stared at the bastard who'd forced Mitch to distance himself from his wife and daughter for their own protection.

"Ah, I see you recognize my name. Good. Then you know I'm not a man to be crossed. I'll speak with you at lunch, Lieutenant."

I didn't try to stop him this time. I watched him disappear in to the cool, dim interior while Aviator Glasses let himself out the front door. That left me face-to-face

146

with the brunette. She and I measured each other for several long seconds.

I could take her, I decided. She had several inches on me but those were all heel. And odds were she'd never done a push-up in her life.

Not that I've done all that many. The recently implemented Air Force aerobics program requires a minimum of a mile-and-a-half run, eighteen push-ups, and thirty-eight sit-ups for women in my age group. I'm still working my way up to the minimum. But I *could* put a heavy-soled combat boot to her gut and knock her flat on her behind.

Then what?

I still didn't know where I was, although I was pretty certain now it wasn't Arizona or New Mexico. My guess was that I was well south of the border.

Nor did I know what Mendoza wanted with me, but I guessed with sick certainty that it involved Mitch. I needed to find out what the rat bastard was up to before deciding on a plan of action.

"All right, Teresa. You heard the man." I flicked a careless hand. "Lead the way."

Despite the powder puff shoes, she was no dummy. She wasn't about to let me walk behind her, get her in a stranglehold, and snap her neck. With an abrupt gesture, she indicated I should precede her.

"Go through the salons."

Her English wasn't as polished as Mendoza's but still light years ahead of my Spanish.

"What do you do here?" I asked as I took the lead.

"I am the *patron*'s executive assistant."

Suuure she was.

"I noticed he wears a wedding ring." *And you don't.* "Is his wife here, too?"

"No."

The single syllable cracked like a whip. Obviously, I'd struck a nerve.

"So this place is, what?" I said, digging the spur in deeper. "Mendoza's hideaway when he wants to get away from the missus?"

"Take the hall to your right," she said, ignoring my question.

I tried to memorize the function and layout of the rooms we passed. The two salons, one with a sunken conversation pit; a high-tech office bristling with electronics; a home theater; a dining room with sliding glass doors that looked out over the mesa; an inner atrium that appeared to have no other purpose than to show off another bronze sculpture. This one had to be at least fifteen or twenty feet tall. I'm not as familiar with kachinas as I should be after so many months in the southwest, but I thought it was the lizard god.

"Take the stairs to your left," Teresa instructed.

The flagstone steps led down to a short corridor that ended in a carved wooden door. I stopped and waited while she punched a wall keypad. When the electronic lock clicked open, she gestured me into a self-contained suite.

If not for that keypad, I might have mistaken this for an elegant guest suite. A flat-screen TV hung on one wall. On the other was an antique mirror flanked by exquisite pierced-tin lanterns. No phone anywhere in sight, though.

My initial impression had been right, I saw as I glanced around. The house *was* carved out of the mesa. This suite was obviously below ground level. The only natural light came from a single row of glass blocks set high in the wall. Too high to reach without something tall and heavy to stand on. And way too narrow to wiggle through.

The hum I'd heard earlier sounded closer, as though it emanated from just outside the glass blocks. "There are clothes in the closet, fresh towels in the bath," Teresa informed me. "I'll come for you when it's time for lunch."

The door thudded shut. The lock clicked into place a second later.

I stood where I was, trying to decide my next move. Gut instinct told me the room was bugged. Probably with both audio and video. No way I was giving Mendoza's boys a peep show by stripping down to shower and/or change clothes. Nor was I the least inclined to shed my ABUs and boots. I've complained about both often enough but at that moment I derived considerable consolation from the fact that my uniform represented the full might of the United States' military establishment.

Too bad I didn't have some means of signaling that establishment to call in an air strike or artillery barrage. But my purse was nowhere in sight and a check of my various pockets confirmed they'd been emptied. Even the twenty I routinely tucked in a leg pocket for emergencies was gone.

With nothing else to do, I went into the bathroom to soap my bloody wrist, wash my face, and rake a hand through my hair. Then I sat down on the edge of the bed to wait.

I waited for several hours. Mendoza obviously keeps Continental hours. The kind I used to keep when I hustled drinks at the casino. Breakfast at nine or ten. A light lunch before heading to work at four. Dinner either snatched during a midnight break or with friends after I got off.

Considerably different from my present regimen. Meal hours at officer training school were such a shock to my system I barely ate for the first three days. Now I've become so conditioned to the dawn/noon/early evening routine that my stomach starts making nasty noises if I miss any of the designated times.

It started talking to me as I sat there on the bed, reminding me it had missed its dawn feeding. Which made me think of the French crullers and lemon-filled I'd tossed aside in my frantic attempt to hit the right panic button. Which in turn made me wonder if anyone had seen the scuffle in the parking lot.

And what happened to my key ring with the FBI's handy-dandy little tracking device? Had I dropped it beside my car? Or had Pipe Guy picked it up and pocketed it? If so, Paul Donati and company might've tracked him down and beat my present location out of him. Maybe they were already winging their way to the high mesa.

Hope leaped so hard and fast into my throat I almost choked on it. Just as quickly, I gulped it back down. For all I knew, the key ring had flown out of my hand with the donuts and got left behind in the parking lot. In that case Paul—and Mitch and my team—would know I'd gone missing but wouldn't know why or where. I couldn't base my plan of attack on unknowns.

That, of course, begged the question of what I *could* base it on. At this point I was clueless. All I could do was ignore the increasingly obnoxious noises emanating from my midsection and wait.

Since I don't wear a watch and rely on my cell phone to check the time, I estimated it was a good two hours before Slut Shoes returned.

Teresa. Her name was Teresa. I'd better remember that if I was going to worm information out of her.

"So, Teresa," I let drop as we went up the stairs, "it doesn't scare you to climb into a small plane and zoom in for a landing on top of a big rock?"

No response.

"It sure caught my attention. Taking off over those sheer cliffs has to be even scarier."

Still no reply. So much for my unsubtle attempt to verify how ordinary mortals got off this rock. But I was sure there had to be a road cut into the mesa. No plane small enough to land atop it could airlift in that three-ton Hummer. And what came up, I thought grimly as Teresa gestured me through an archway, could go down.

I received visual confirmation of that when we stepped through the sliding glass doors to a flagstone patio. The sun still beat down, but a soft wind stirred the leaves of the twisted mesquite shading the patio and kept the afternoon heat at bay.

The temperature didn't interest me as much as the view from the patio. It was set high enough for a clear view beyond the encircling wall. The road that trailed toward the edge of the mesa was hardly more than a dirt track, but it had to lead somewhere! And there, parked beside an adobe garage about fifty yards from the main house, was the Hummer.

My mind clicked like a camera shutter, fixing every detail in my mind before I switched my attention to the buffet set out on the patio. Dome-topped serving dishes displayed raw oysters on the half shell, bright pink shrimp nested on ice, and some greenish, slug-like things I wanted no part of. The heavyset female adding a bowl of ceviche to the table eyed me curiously before disappearing through the door to what I assumed was the kitchen.

Took me a moment to locate Mendoza. He was seated in the shade of the mesquite at a table set with colorful linen, perusing some kind of legal document. In his open-necked silk shirt and pleated pants he looked as relaxed and comfortable as I was tight and wary.

He glanced up at our approach and hiked a brow. "I see you decided not to change into something cooler."

"I prefer my uniform."

Especially if I had to make a quick escape.

"As you wish," Mendoza said with a shrug. "Please, have a seat."

I took a chair on the other side of the table. I wanted

to keep this guy in full view. Teresa started to pull out the chair next to him, but Mendoza stopped her by handing her the document.

"Take this into the office, my pet. I'll join you there after lunch and finish going through it."

The casual dismissal sent a tinge of red into her cheeks, but she accepted the document and left without a word.

Her boss-slash-lover didn't give her a second look. Playing the gracious host, he extracted a bottle from the ice bucket on the table.

"Would you care for wine with lunch, Lieutenant? This is a very good chenin blanc from the Valle de Guadalupe that you might . . ."

"No."

"Very well." Unperturbed, he resettled the bottle. "Shall we dine first, then talk?"

"Let's talk now," I said, ignoring the instant shriek of protest from my stomach. "Why am I here, Mendoza?"

His eyes narrowed. My palms got a little clammy as I recalled his previous order to address him with respect, but I refused to tack on a "mister" or "señor."

"You don't take instruction well, do you, Lieutenant?"

Despite the chalky taste of fear in my mouth, I worked up a sardonic smile. "Funny, that's what my boss always says."

The ice in Mendoza's eyes gave way to a look of surprise, followed by a slight gleam of appreciation.

"You're not very wise, but you have courage. I see now why Mitchell has taken such an interest in you."

My last desperate hope this didn't involve some

scheme to get at Mitch died. Mendoza's next comment pounded the nails into its coffin.

"That interest has provided me the means to an end I've waited a long time to achieve."

"I don't know what you're talking about," I lied.

"Surely Special Agent Mitchell has told you that he caused me great inconvenience some years ago? I had to spend considerable money and effort to rectify the situation. Now it's time to balance the sheet."

I couldn't believe this guy! He might have been talking about a stock deal gone bad. Yet I knew damned well he'd made millions trading in every form of human misery.

Mitch had come face-to-face with one facet of Mendoza's operation when he'd intercepted a truckload of human cargo destined for a brothel in Houston. They were just kids, he'd told me grimly. Some not more than eight or ten years old. Scared to death and crying for their mamas. Merchandise in a well-organized and obscenely profitable human smuggling ring.

A father himself, Mitch had been sickened by what he saw and volunteered to work with a friend in Mexico as part of a cross-border task force. Took them months, but they finally tracked the ring to Mendoza. They'd hauled him in and testified at his trial in Mexico City, but bribes and jury intimidation got the man off. The youngest son of Mitch's counterpart disappeared a month later. Although the police could never tie the abduction to Mendoza, Mitch knew it was done out of revenge, pure and simple.

At that point his already disintegrating marriage had come apart at the seams. Railing at him for putting his job ahead of his family, his wife had insisted he set up a safe haven for her and their daughter as far from El Paso as they could get.

Mendoza hadn't found them. Now, apparently, he'd decided he didn't have to.

"I don't see what your problems with Mitch have to do with me," I said with a carelessness I was far from feeling. "He and I are friends, but . . ."

"Please, Lieutenant. Don't play the fool. I know very well you're more than friends. I sent someone to watch you shortly after your name and photograph were splashed all over the news last week."

"Why? Was that slime, Victor Duarte, one of your pals?"

"Duarte?" He showed his teeth in shark's smile. "On the contrary. Duarte did that job for one of my rivals. The killings severely disrupted my midwestern operation. If you hadn't eliminated Duarte, I would have."

"So why did you have me watched?"

"The device the media said you were testing intrigued me. I saw some interesting potential applications for it."

Well, damn! I'd tossed that possibility at Paul Donati as a wild guess but I hadn't really given it much credence. Mendoza just made a believer out of me.

"I had Teresa go online to research both you and the device," he continued. "She found a number of articles about you written prior to the Duarte incident. You appear to attract trouble, Lieutenant."

I didn't bother to tell him he was quoting my boss again. Nor did I care for the lethal satisfaction that slid into his voice.

"Imagine my surprise—and delight—when one of those articles linked you to Jeff Mitchell and a case he'd worked. I decided to send a man to check you out and knew I'd hit the jackpot when he saw Mitchell arrive at your place *very* early last Saturday morning."

I sensed it was helpless at this point, but I still tried to put a spike in whatever Mendoza had planned.

"Then your goon saw me drive him home to change a little later. After which I took him to the airport. Mitch needed a ride, that's all."

"Really? Well, we'll soon see."

With another snarky smile, he picked up a small, serrated knife. The kind with sharp prongs on the tip that you can use to pry open oysters. When he shoved back his chair and started for me, I jumped up.

"What . . . ?" I wet my lips and backed away, my heart hammering. "What the hell do you think you're going to do with that?"

"Cut off a small piece of you to send Agent Mitchell."

CHAPTER TWELVE

THIS was, hands down, my worst nightmare! I'd stumbled into some desperate situations before but I'd never had someone like Rafael Mendoza come at me with an oyster knife.

I lunged back and would have tripped over my chair if he hadn't leaped forward and caught my wildly windmilling arm.

"Be careful!"

Careful, hell! With my feet under me again, I balled my other fist and rammed the heel at his nose. He jerked to the side, narrowly dodging the blow. Since he still had my arm in an iron grip, he jerked me with him.

"Be still, you stupid *puta*! You'll hurt yourself."

"Or you will."

Snarling, I yanked at my arm like a cougar with its

foreleg caught in a trap. Mendoza muttered a vicious oath and released it.

"I'm not going to cut you."

I wasn't taking his word for that. Panting, I put the chair between us.

"That's not what you said a minute ago."

I was calculating the odds I could snatch up the chair and smash it down on his head when he curled his lip.

"*Cristo!* Did you think I intended to send Mitchell a finger or an ear?"

What the heck else was I supposed to think after watching so many *Godfather* movies and *Sopranos* reruns? I was extremely relieved to hear Mendoza didn't subscribe to their modus operandi, but my relief lasted all of two seconds.

"It may come to that," he said with a sneer. "For now, I want only your tape."

"My what?"

He gestured impatiently at my chest with the tip of the knife. "The piece with your name."

I glanced down at the name tape just above my breast pocket.

"It's sewn on," I said stupidly.

Well, duh! He could see how it was attached as well as I could. At least now I understood why he'd come at me with a sharp-tipped oyster knife.

"Give me the knife. I'll cut it off."

The man was either supremely confident of his own abilities or completely disdainful of mine. Reversing the knife, he held it out by the handle.

I took it and considered stabbing the blade into his

throat or eye for all of two seconds. No point attacking the man when he was prepared for it. He'd already proved his reflexes were as good or better than mine.

My hands shook as I slid the short, sharp pick under a corner of the tape. The tailors on post used heavy-duty thread to attach these name tapes. Probably so they wouldn't catch on a sharp protrusion while the wearer is on patrol or come off after repeated launderings. I popped several stitches and freed one end but couldn't get a good grip.

Mendoza made impatient noises while I tugged at the tape, then shoved my hand aside and ripped it away from my chest. Stupid, I know, but the act made me feel so violated that my grip on the knife turned my fingers white to the bone.

The look that leaped into Medoza's eyes stopped me before I brought the knife up in a swift arc. He *wanted* me to go for him. *Wanted* the thrill of subduing me. The bastard got off on violence.

Sure enough, I detected both disappointment and mockery on his face as he raised his voice. "Anna Maria!"

The sturdy woman I'd glimpsed earlier hurried from the kitchen. *"Si, patron?"*

Mendoza handed her the tape and issued rapid-fire orders in Spanish. I understood only a few words but *aeroplano* suggested Aviator Glasses would soon climb back into his aircraft and wing his way north. I didn't know how or when the tape would be delivered to Mitch. My stomach cramped when I thought of the message that would accompany it.

"Now we will eat," Mendoza said when the cook or

maid or whatever she was hurried off. "Sit down, Lieutenant."

I came damned close to telling Mendoza to take his oysters and shove 'em, shells and all. I refrained, however. I couldn't engineer an escape or make it across miles of desert weak with hunger.

That was my rationale anyway as I filled a plate with shrimp and ceviche and baby asparagus topped with a white sauce so thick and rich it almost wouldn't dribble from the serving spoon. I added two warm, puffy flour tortillas and a slab of butter before returning to the table.

"You live well here on your mountaintop," I commented when Mendoza resumed his seat as well.

"Yes, I do." He poured himself another glass of wine. "I have homes in Mexico City and Playa del Carmen, but my roots are here in the high desert. I come back as often as possible."

"Where, exactly, is here?"

"Too far from civilization for you to survive if you try to escape, Lieutenant."

"Then tell me this. How long do you intend to keep me here?"

His dark eyes met mine across the rim of his glass. "As long as necessary."

I forced down a forkful of spicy ceviche and decided to forego conversation for the rest of the meal. Mendoza decided otherwise.

"Tell me more about this device you and your team tested. The one that causes such a furor with the media. Does it really convert natural sources to energy?"

I pasted Mendoza's face on the mental image of a kangaroo rat and smiled. "It does."

"How close is the military to moving from a prototype to full production?"

Obviously he'd never delved into the procurement cycle for military systems. Research and development alone could take decades, testing various prototypes another five years.

Unless the country was at war, of course. Then the development cycle shortened in direct proportion to the urgency of the need. I had yet to convince Dr. J that Snoopy could fill some of the military's very urgent needs, but that ranked near the top of my to-do list when I got back.

If I got back.

THAT big, fat "if" hovered front and center in my mind throughout the remainder of a long afternoon confined to the guest suite. I spent a good part of that time stretched out atop the downy comforter on the king-sized bed, my fingers laced behind my head while I contemplated my options. I didn't see many. Zero, in fact.

Driven to desperation, I finally stabbed the remote and fired up the flat-screen TV. It had to be close to news time. With any luck I would find a local station with a weather forecaster doing his thing in front of a map with towns and cities that might pinpoint my location.

What I found were hundreds of local stations. With newscasters speaking dozens of different languages. In twenty different time zones. Damned satellite TV.

I was about to give my thumb a rest when a familiar logo flashed up on the screen. Thank God! That was Channel Nine, El Paso!

I shot up in bed as a familiar anchor announced that they were going live for an update with their reporter on the scene. A second later, Junior Reporter's face filled the scene.

"In the latest in a bizarre series of incidents," he intoned, "it appears that Lieutenant Samantha Spade has been abducted. As you may recall, she is the Air Force officer involved in the shooting less than a week ago of the man, Victor Duarte, alleged to have decapitated three men."

My image replaced Junior Reporter's. An official photo this time. Not the wild-eyed shot he'd dug out of the archives for his first story.

"Her abandoned vehicle was found early this morning at a strip mall across the street from Fort Bliss's Cassidy Gate. The FBI is asking anyone who might have spotted Lieutenant Spade or her abductors to contact them immediately."

The scene cut back to Junior Reporter. His face solemn above his navy blue blazer, DeWayne looked straight into the camera. No doubt about it. His days of covering high school track-and-field were behind him.

"Authorities refuse to confirm whether Lieutenant Spade's disappearance is related to the shooting or, as this reporter suspects, to the self-nurturing refueling device she and her team were testing for the Department of Defense. Or, perhaps, the super-secret signal diffuser

Lieutenant Spade's senior test engineer insisted they were *not* testing when I interviewed him earlier this afternoon."

Huh? What super-secret signal diffuser?

I scooted to the end of the bed, my jaw sagging as Rocky's image replaced DeWayne's. He was standing on the steps of our office building. That meant the Fort Bliss Public Affairs Office had granted DeWayne and his camera crew on-post access.

But why the heck had Rocky agreed to talk to them? He generally avoided the media like the plague. I suspected his aversion to the spotlight might have something to do with the eyebrow-less scientist at DARPA headquarters.

But there he was, palming his sandy hair and looking as though he might let loose with one of his bloopers. For their sakes, I hoped Junior Reporter and his cameraman weren't within striking distance.

"I don't know where you people get your information," he said testily. "Or in this case, misinformation. I can state categorically that no one has submitted a signal diffuser for our evaluation. And if they had, I wouldn't discuss such sensitive technology on camera."

"But that's the issue in a nutshell, Dr. Balboa. Why is this information so sensitive? My sources tell me the diffuser is little more than a TV remote with its receptor boosted to such an extent that it scrambles satellite signals and bounces them back to the station that broadcast them."

"Please." Rocky looked as pained as a thin, nervous little twitch could. "What you're talking about requires a Nyquist filter carrier recovery circuit, a mixer, a level shifter, and a preemphasis circuit for transmitting scrambled TV-IF signals on an FM or digital link."

"Huh?"

That one came from DeWayne, not me. He recovered after a few seconds of dead air.

"So there's no way for Joe Six-Pack, sitting in his recliner in front of his TV, to play with his remote and boost the TV's signals?"

"None, unless he has access to the items I just mentioned. And a Big Red Shield."

"A what?"

"That, sir, *is* classified."

"Yes, but . . ."

Rocky swallowed and set his Adam's apple to bobbing. I recognized the warning signs and froze. I had a good idea what might happen next.

Sure enough, Junior Reporter's voice faltered and his eyes popped. "Wh . . . ? What . . . ?"

He choked, and I grimaced in sympathy as the camera tilted and displayed a wide swath of sky. Listeners were treated to the sound of scuffling in the background before Junior Reporter gasped into the mike.

"This is . . . DeWayne Wilson, reporting for . . . Channel Nine News."

The scene switched back to the newsroom. The anchor looked surprised but launched into her next story. I didn't hear a word she said.

I sat like a lump of lava rock and stared sightlessly at the screen. That bizarre exchange told me Rocky and Mitch and the rest of the gang didn't have a clue where

I was. They were grasping at straws, feeding the press—and anyone else who might be listening—misinformation. A sick feeling rolled aorund in my belly at the idea I might never see any of them again.

Even worse, Mendoza had used me as bait for his long-delayed revenge. I knew Mitch. He wouldn't hesitate. He'd take any risks, face any odds, to get to me.

I slapped a hand to my chest where my name tape had been and fingered the loose threads, feeling even sicker. Took a while for a glimmer of reason to work its way through the despair that fogged my head and my heart.

That was Rocky on TV. Taciturn, oddball Rocky. He would never get in front of a camera unless driven by sheer desperation.

But he hadn't looked desperate. Only annoyed at Boy Reporter for harping on about this . . . What had DeWayne called it? Super secret signal defuser?

Okay! All right! I shook my head to clear the fog. What the heck had Rock been trying to tell me? I replayed the interview again in my mind. Was he suggesting I could rig a device to boost satellite TV signals and bounce them back to the source? That he and the team could somehow intercept those signals?

Or . . .

Omigod! A Big Red Shield!

I had a sudden vision of Charlie's crestfallen expression when he explained that all he'd done was insert a tiny slip of foil-backed paper from his Big Red in the Amorphic Cube's control unit. He had no idea the unit would supercharge and blow our building's entire electrical system.

I sat on the end of the bed, oblivious to the commercial now blaring from the screen as I gripped the TV remote. All I could hear was the faint hum of the generators outside the glass block windows.

We used generators at our test site for backup power for thc lab. As far as I could tell, they provided the *only* source of power here on the rock. If I could jam their controls, shut them down . . .

I tried to remember how the heck the generators at the site worked. Sergeant Cassidy usually took care of fueling and servicing them. I was pretty sure, though, they operated on an automatic switch. One sensitive enough to power fluctuations that they would automatically kick on if we lost our main power source. If these suckers were half as sensitive . . .

I tried to control my rush of excitement by staring fixedly at the screen. All the while I formulated and rejected various schemes for obtaining a strip of tinfoil.

IT turned out to be surprisingly easy.

All I had to do was wait for Teresa to come fetch me again. She'd changed for dinner. The slim skirt and powder-puff shoes were gone. In their place she wore gold thong sandals with hourglass-shaped heels and a lavender, off-one-shoulder dress.

Her lip curled as she took in my military haute couture. "Why do you not wear something more comfortable?"

I jettisoned all attempts to get friendly with her, since

they weren't working anyway. "Why do you not take a running jump off the high end of the mesa?"

Her mouth tightened. "Go!"

I started up the stone steps. Halfway to the upper landing, I put a hand against the wall and leaned into it for a moment.

"What's the matter?" she asked sharply.

"Nothing," I said, every bit as sharp, and pushed away from the wall.

We turned left at the top of the stairs and passed the doors to the patio where Mendoza and I had had lunch. A bouquet of sizzling pork and spicy sauce emanated from the short hallway that led to the kitchen.

Teresa trailed me into a dining room with lustrous dark wood beams, a red-tiled floor, and a massive, refectory-style table that looked as though it might have come from an old Spanish mission. The table was set with gold-rimmed china and crystal that sparkled in the light from a four-tiered chandelier with Tiffany shades in glowing desert hues. I noted three place settings and couldn't resist twisting the knife a bit.

"Are you being allowed to eat at the grown-ups' table tonight?"

"Sit!"

I reached for the high-backed wooden chair she indicated with a terse wave of her hand and went into my act again. Hanging onto the chair, I bent at the waist and made a low, inarticulate sound.

"What is it?" she asked with a quick frown.

"I don't know." I straightened, breathing heavily. "I've

been feeling woozy. Could be the aftereffects of that stuff your friends pumped into me."

"Sit down, and it may pass."

"I don't think so. I need to lie down. I'd better go back downstairs."

"Very well."

"I was too nervous to eat at lunch," I lied as we retraced our steps. "It may help if I could put something in my stomach."

"I will have Anna Maria bring you a plate," Teresa said impatiently.

"Isn't that the kitchen?"

"You do not need to go . . ."

Too late. I'd already navigated the short corridor. Rounding a corner, I entered a kitchen decorated with bright tiles and ropes of dried chilies. My darting glance locked immediately on the cordless phone nestled in its cradle on the tiled counter. My heart pumped, but I knew it would be useless to make a grab for it. Teresa was just a half step behind.

Besides, there were two women in the kitchen. One was the stout Anna Maria. She stood behind a tiled cooktop, stirring the contents of saucepan. Another, younger woman was in the act of removing an oval pan containing a sizzling roast from the oven. A monster pork roast browned to perfection and protected by a tented piece of foil!

Both women looked up, startled by our entrance. While Teresa explained our presence in rapid Spanish, I mentally rehearsed my lines.

"Anna Maria asks what you wish to eat?" my escort translated impatiently.

"A few slices of that pork and some of the tortillas we had at lunch." I wrapped an arm across my waist and feigned a gag. "Just ask her to fix a plate and cover it with foil to keep the food hot. I'm not sure how much I can keep down right now."

"They will bring it to you," Teresa said hastily, obviously afraid I would puke all over the kitchen.

ONCE back in my luxurious cell, I stretched out on the bed and counted the minutes until dinner arrived. By then my stomach was churning so much acid that I didn't have to pretend wooziness.

Anna Maria deposited the tray on the bedside table, answered my attempts to engage her in conversation with a shake of her head, and returned to kitchen. The tray didn't include a knife, I saw at a glance, or fork for that matter. Nothing I might use as a weapon.

Swallowing my disappointment, I played to any unseen cameras by rolling a piece of pork in a tortilla and taking a bite. My face puckered. My eyes scrunched. Groaning, I returned the wrap to the plate and covered it. In the process, I tore off a tiny strip of foil.

Then I stretched out again and waited. Thirty minutes. An hour. Two.

I kept expecting Mendoza to send Teresa to check on me. Or come himself to tell me the name tape he'd ripped from my uniform had been delivered.

Then again, I reasoned, his real focus was Mitch. He'd made it painfully clear I was merely a pawn in his brutal game, a means to an end. And if Mendoza could get a line on Snoopy SNFIR in the process, it would just be a nice bonus. He had no need to keep me apprised on his progress on either front.

If Mitch had received the tape, I was sure he wouldn't release that information to the media, but I tuned in to the late night news anyway. Neither Mitch nor Paul Donati made an appearance. Junior Reporter's eager face came on the screen, though. To my disappointment he merely rehashed the same information he'd broadcast earlier and showed a condensed version of his interview with Rocky.

I clutched the remote in a sweaty palm, praying I hadn't fantasized Rocky's hidden message, and pretended to drift into a restless sleep.

CHAPTER THIRTEEN

I'D purposely left both the bedside lamp and the TV on. They provided more than sufficient light when I pushed groggily to my feet in the still of the night and stumbled for the bathroom. But not enough, I sincerely hoped, to provide any unseen watchers a view of me sitting on the john—or jacking off the rear panel of the TV remote.

I was so nervous I broke a nail prying out the four AAA batteries. I didn't take time to mourn the loss. Hand shaking, I wedged the tiny strip of foil under the metal contacts and reinserted the batteries. That done, I made a show of stumbling back to the bed.

I stretched out with my hands clasped loosely on my belly, holding the remote with seeming nonchalance. My heart zinged around inside my chest as I pressed the power switch. I kept the pressure on, squeezing hard, while aiming the signal at the row of glass blocks above the TV.

Honestly? I didn't really believe this jerry-rigged signal booster would work. The remote was getting warm, though. I could feel the heat through the plastic casing. My heart thumped harder and faster as I feigned a semi-doze and squeezed the power button for all I was worth.

The heat intensified. My thumb joint started to ache from the unceasing pressure. Every muscle in my body strained with the effort of maintaining my slumberous pose while waiting for something—anything!—to happen.

The TV went first. The picture flickered. The characters in the late night Western blurred. Then, with a small pop, the volume cut off and the flat screen went black.

Yes!

I kept the pressure on, hard and tight. Pain radiated from my thumb to my wrist. The remote's casing got so hot that I expected to smell melting plastic and/or sizzling flesh at any moment.

With the sound from the TV cut off, the faint hum outside the window seemed louder. Steadier. Mocking me. Mocking my ridiculous attempts to . . .

Oh, God! Was that a burp?

A hiccup in the low, steady pulse?

Before I could answer my own, desperate question, the hum cut off completely. In the same heartbeat, the bedside lamp died. My subterranean chamber plunged into darkness so profound that my suddenly diminished senses almost missed the faint click across the room.

The electronic door lock! I hadn't expected it to pop when the generators went. I'd thought I would have to wait until Teresa or one of Mendoza's security guys came to check on me and fight my way out.

Change of plans. I was off the bed and running for the door before my eyes had fully adjusted to the darkness. I slammed into the wall, swore viciously under my breath, and fumbled for the door handle. It gave, and I hit the flagstone steps.

Enough moonlight filtered through the upstairs windows for me to see where I was going, thank God! I didn't bounce off any more walls and in the few moments it took me to reach the kitchen I conducted a fierce debate. I could grab the phone I'd spotted there, make a frantic call, hope Mitch or Paul Donati could pinpoint the location of the call, hotfoot it back to my cell before anyone knew I was on the loose, and wait for rescue.

Or I get the hell out of Dodge.

As I'm sure you've surmised by now, I'm not the waiting-for-rescue type. Nor was I all that sure I could make the call and get back to my room undetected. That was my rationale, anyway, for hitting the kitchen on a dead run and swooping the phone from its cradle.

I swooped up several other items as well. One was a dishtowel hanging on a rack beside the sink. Cramming it and the phone in a leg pocket, I yanked open the stainless steel fridge and fumbled in its inky darkness. I almost sobbed with relief when my searching hand closed around cold, crinkly plastic. Three icy water bottles went into my other pockets. Swearing that I would never complain about my baggy ABUs again, I bolted for the kitchen's back door.

With even an ounce of luck, I would hightail it off this rock and make it to civilization before dawn. If so, I wouldn't need either the water or the towel to protect my neck and head from the daytime sun. But I'd lived and worked in West Texas long enough to have a healthy respect for the high desert. I wasn't leaving this mesa either by vehicle or on foot unprepared.

As I grabbed the kitchen's door handle, I did a huge mental finger-cross. I had no idea if the exterior perimeter was alarmed and if so, whether the alarm system had emergency backup battery power separate from the generators.

My luck held! I shot through the door and into the star-studded night without a single siren wail. Dodging clumps of feathery pampas grass and the artistically arranged rocks landscaping the rear of the house, I made for the garage I'd spotted at lunch. My boots hit the winding, hard-packed dirt path, each thud sounding like a rifle shot as I ran for the Hummer still parked beside the garage. I'd pretty well used up my supply of luck but I begged God for one more favor. Just one more. Please! Let it be unlocked.

Okay, two more. Let it be unlocked and the keys be in the ignition.

It was, but they weren't. Panting, I yanked down the visor. Thrust a hand under the seat. Thumped my palm frantically across the dash. I'd picked up a fair number of skills during my two years in uniform. Hot-wiring a Hummer wasn't one of them.

I'd almost given up and decided to make a run for it when I spotted the keys lying right there in the driver's seat.

Thank you, Lord!

I hopped in and hopped right out again. All those episodes of *The Sopranos* had taught me a few things, too. Hefting a rock, I smashed the Hummer's taillights. No point making it easy for the bad guys to follow me.

I jumped back in the vehicle and cranked it up. To my intense relief, it was an H2 with automatic and four-wheel drive. At least I wouldn't have to up- and down-shift all the way to the bottom of the mesa.

If I made it to the bottom of the mesa. That became somewhat doubtful when I heard a shout and jerked my head around. The dark figure that came running from the house had me shoving the Hummer into gear and stomping on the gas. I didn't turn on the headlights. I couldn't see the switch in the darkness and didn't have time to look for it. Especially not after a loud crack spilt the night—and shattered the rear window!

Thankfully, I could see the dirt track leading to the rear of the mesa clearly in the moonlight. I *didn't* see the terrifyingly steep angle the track took until I hit the mesa's edge.

"Shit!"

I yanked the wheel and somehow kept the heavy tank of a vehicle from sailing into dark, empty space. Drenched in the acrid sweat of terror I got all four wheels back on the dirt track again.

I had to put the headlights on then. The track was in shadow and too damned narrow to navigate by the light of the moon. I kept one hand on the wheel and used the other to twist every knob within reach until twin beams stabbed through the night.

As soon as they came on, I yanked the cordless phone out of my leg pocket. I didn't know how powerful it was. Or whether this rapid descent would block its signal. Or whether my homemade jammer had scrambled its transmissions, too!

Keeping one eye on the steep track and one eye on the phone, I stabbed in a number I knew almost as well as my own and jammed the instrument to my ear. I couldn't decide whether to shout with joy or sob with relief when I heard it ring. Once. Twice. I was praying again by the third. Almost weeping by the fourth.

I'd yanked the phone away from my ear to try a different number when I heard a terse, "Mitchell."

"Mitch! It's me."

"Samantha! Are you all right?"

I didn't have time to list all the ways I *wasn't* all right.

"Yes."

"Where the hell are you?"

"I don't know. Somewhere in Mexico." The words tumbled out, fast and furious. "I'm in high desert, so I know I've got to be east of the Sierra Madre Occidental."

Thank you, Pen!

(I'd never heard of the Sierra Madre Occidental before her lengthy discourse on the subject.)

"It's Mendoza, Mitch. He took me."

"That's what I figured."

The hard, flat reply told me he'd received my name

tape and whatever message Mendoza had sent with it.

"I have to talk fast," I said breathlessly. "I stole a Hummer. I'm careening down from a high mesa, and this phone may cut off at any moment."

Or Mendoza's goons could be on my tail. I threw a frantic glance in the rearview mirror. Nothing. Yet.

"I'll keep the phone on. Try to get a lock on its signal."

"It's already in progress. Donati put a tap on my phones right after you disappeared, in case you tried to get hold of me."

Thank you, Paul!

"I'm heading north. I think. Toward the border."

"Don't cut across the desert," Mitch warned sharply. "We've found too many abandoned vehicles mired in the sand or nose-down in gullies."

With dead or dying victims nearby. He didn't give me the latest head count. He didn't have to. It made the news regularly on both sides of the border.

"I'll get . . . ati . . ."

Oh, no! Not already!

"Mitch," I almost cried into the phone, "you're breaking up!"

"Don't . . . up. I . . . find you."

The line went dead on the fierce promise of those last two words. I took a big gulp of air and clung to the memory of the experimental device we'd tested last year that could raise signals from dead cell phones. The technology for that device hadn't made it into the commercial marketplace yet, but the Border Patrol was part of the Department of Homeland Security. They—and the FBI—had access to all kinds of whoo-whoo gadgets.

Dropping the phone on the passenger seat, I held on to Mitch's promise with the same ferocity I gripped the steering wheel. The tension racing up and down my spine lessened only marginally when I took the last turn and the steep incline flattened.

A dirt track stretched straight ahead, like a pale ribbon banded on both sides by the darker shades of the desert. I muttered a fervent prayer and floored the Hummer. I'd gone maybe two hundred yards when I caught a flash of light in the rearview mirror.

Headlights. Two laser-like beams. Stabbing the night sky behind and above me. Making me wish to hell I'd had time to break into the garage and disable whatever other vehicles Mendoza kept in his stable.

The beams' angle indicated my pursuers were only halfway down the mesa. That gave me at best a ten-minute lead. And five seconds to weigh the odds that the heavy Hummer could outrun whatever they were driving.

Not bloody likely! These suckers were built for durability, not speed. I sucked air, killed the headlights, kicked into four wheel drive and did exactly what Mitch had warned me not to.

One wrench of the wheel sent the Hummer off the track. It rocketed across the rough earth, flattening a cholla and humping over a prairie dog mound before I regained control. I had to wait for a relatively unencumbered stretch to risk a quick glance over my shoulder.

"Ha!" I flipped a mental finger at the distant spear of lights. "Catch me if you can, you bastards."

Wrenching my gaze forward again, I gave the desert every ounce of concentration. My best hope—my only hope—lay in covering as much distance as possible before dawn broke and showed Mendoza and company where I'd left the road.

THAT was the plan, anyway. It might have worked, too, if I hadn't sent the Hummer into a dry gulch. It hit sideways, two wheels fighting to grab the bank, two wheels sinking into nothingness. I fought the steep pitch but couldn't get level. The sour taste of fear filled my throat as the heavy vehicle tipped onto its side and started to roll.

Dumb idea to drive across the desert without lights, I thought on a flash of sheer panic. Reeeeally dumb.

The driver's side slammed into the rock-hard bank. My head slammed into the side window. The airbag exploded in my face. Bright yellow stars spun in front of my eyes, and the coppery taste of blood filled my mouth.

When the stars faded, I was still strapped in but my seat was now horizontal. I wiggled tentatively and confirmed that all my moving parts still worked. The pain, I concluded, came from whacking my head against the window, the blood from biting my lower lip when the air bag punched into me.

Grimacing, I dragged my tongue over the raw, bleeding patch and fumbled for the seat belt release. Took a few tries but I finally managed to push up the passenger side door and haul myself through the opening.

The effort left me so dizzy and disoriented I almost blacked out. I spread both feet and forced myself to breathe slow and deep until the dizziness passed.

Okay. All right. Time for plan B. Or C. Or whatever I was up to at this point.

"Think, Spade," I muttered, willing my rattled brain back to full operation. "Think."

I wasn't worried about tackling the desert on foot. Pen had drummed volumes of information into my unwilling head with her lectures. Sergeant Cassidy had contributed some extremely useful but not particularly appetizing tidbits, as well. Special Ops types live, eat, sleep, and operate in some really gross situations.

Mitch had also shared stories about people whose cars or trucks had broken down while they were trying to sneak across the border. In that situation, conventional wisdom said to stay with your vehicle and spread every loose object you had with your around the car's exterior so it could be spotted more easily from the air.

Conventional wisdom presupposed, of course, that you didn't have a slime like Mendoza on the hunt for you. A slime who could call in his own light plane to aid in the search. I knew I had to make tracks before Aviator Glasses arrived on the scene.

Correction, I thought with a frown that sent fingers of pain across my brow. The goal was to *not* make tracks.

"Think, Spade. Think."

I had water. A dishtowel to protect my head and neck. Sturdy boots. Pants and a long-sleeved shirt to provide air circulation and keep my sweat from evaporating too quickly. And, I thought as I spotted a piece of the Hummer's broken side mirror, a means of signaling for help. If worse came to absolute worst, I also knew—again courtesy of Pen—which cacti could provide drinkable liquid and which couldn't.

I didn't have the phone, though. That, I discovered when I crawled back inside the Hummer to search for it, had smashed into the instrument panel with the same force with which I'd smashed into the side window. I gathered the pieces on the faint hope Mitch or Paul Donati could trace any residual signals and stuffed then in my pocket.

I wasn't sure how long I had until dawn. Not more than two or three hours, I guessed. Luckily the gully bottom was so dry and cracked that it wouldn't show boot prints. Just to be sure, though, I broke off some creosote limbs and used them as a makeshift broom.

I followed the gully for several hundred yards, sweeping behind me as I went. I continued to sweep after I climbed out. The twisting and bending slowed me down. It also made me dizzy as hell. I kept it up as long as I could but finally had to quit. I could only hope the fragile breeze fluttering the petals of the night-blooming cereus cacti would stir up enough dust to cover my trail from here on out.

I knew I'd overdone it when my temple began to thump with the same rhythm as my boots. Soon every step boomed inside my head like artillery fire. Gritting my teeth, I plowed ahead.

I retained enough clarity to change direction several times. North, then west, then north again. Although high desert nights aren't anywhere near as hot as days, I forced myself to stop and drink at more or less regular intervals. I took full swallows. Tiny sips wouldn't sustain my level of activity. Noel had driven that point home by describing in graphic detail how one of the men in his squad had died of dehydration with a half-full canteen.

When the horizon took on faint shades of pink, I knew I had to find shelter. My head felt as though Slut Shoes was right behind me, beating a meringue on my skull with her four-inch spikes. I dragged on until I spotted some spindly mesquite bent almost to the ground in their desperate attempt to draw moisture from another parched gully.

I could barely place one foot in front of the other by now, but knew I had to put something between the ground and me. When the daytime sun baked the rocks and sand, you didn't need a skillet to fry eggs.

I chose a mesquite that squatted low enough for me to fashion a perch on a fat, twisted branch. My hands shook from exhaustion and pain hammered at me from all sides but I managed to fork two higher branches through the sleeves of my ABU shirt. The fabric's digitized tiger stripes made the improvised canopy almost invisible among the silver and green of the mesquite's leaves.

My standard, yucky brown T-shirt provided little protection as I settled onto my perch and propped my back against the scaly trunk. The dishtowel I draped over my crossed arms to protect them from scratches. The broken mirror piece I slid into the pants pocket closest to hand.

My lids drifted down. I blinked awake. Dozed off again. Jerked and almost tumbled off my branch.

Desperately, I tried to hang onto my balance and my rapidly scattering thoughts.

Mad dogs and Englishmen. Mad dogs and Englishmen. The line kept looping through my fried brain. Don't ask me where I heard it. All I could remember was that it had something to do with the noonday sun.

The phrase was still looping when my chin hit my chest and I blacked out.

CHAPTER FOURTEEN

BELLS? Were those bells?

I kept still, my eyes closed, and tried to determine if that slow, sonorous bonging originated inside or outside my aching head.

Outside, I decided as the deep, resonate sounds knelled again. Definitely outside.

The next challenge was to remember where or when I'd heard them before. I knew I had. Several times. The solemn cadence struck oddly familiar chords. I scrunched my forehead, trying to puzzle it out, and yelped.

"Yowza!"

The pain shot out of nowhere. As sharp and lancing as a spear, it bored into my left temple. I sucked a strangled breath through my nostrils and went stiff as a board.

"*Bueno*. You are awake."

The cheerful voice came at me through the waves of pain and last, echoing bongs. With infinite care, I pried open eyelids that felt as though they'd been glued together.

At first all I saw was a low ceiling showing a spiderweb of cracks. That expanded to include whitewashed walls and four iron bedsteads, one of which I occupied. Then a round, boyish face swam into sight.

"Duwyn?"

Good Lord! Had that hoarse, unintelligible croak come from me? I swiped my tongue over sandpapery lips and tried again.

"DeWayne?"

"DeWayne?" The face hovering over me took on a perplexed look. "What is this DeWayne?"

I had focused enough now to see now this guy wasn't Junior Reporter. Which begged the question . . .

"Who . . . are you?"

The chubby-cheeked stranger broke into a beaming smile. "I am Fay Alfonz."

The grit coating my eyeballs had obviously affected my vision. He didn't look like a she. I swiped my cracked lips again.

"Your name is Fay?"

"No, no! I am *Frey* Alfonz. 'Brother' in your language. Here, let me help you to drink."

Brother? I chewed on that while he slid a hand under my neck. "You're a priest?"

"*Si.*"

There was that joyous smile again. The sheer magnitude of it made my head hurt. I tried to absorb its brilliance in small doses while reflecting on the fact that this chubby-cheeked adolescent didn't resemble any of the friars or priests portrayed in flicks like *The Da Vinci Code* and *Doubt*. Those guys were all pale, ascetic-looking individuals with wooden rosaries dangling from their belts. This friar wore jeans and a frayed T-shirt with faded blue lettering that proclaimed 2008 as *Año de Santo Paulo*.

"How can you be a priest?" I muttered as he raised my head. "You don't look old enough to drink beer, let alone communion wine."

"I add the water to it."

The fingers he slipped around my nape tangled in some strings. Strings to a hospital gown, I realized when I leaned into his hold. One of those open-backed jobbies that afford the medical types easy access and their patient no dignity whatsoever.

When he eased me up, my head flopped onto my shoulder. I couldn't believe how weak I was. And how parched! My entire body shaking, I leaned forward to slurp from the plastic cup he tipped to my lips.

"Slowly," he cautioned. "Drink slowly or you will become sick and disoriented again."

"Again?"

"You have been delirious since Miguel brings you to the clinic."

That explained the whitewashed walls and four beds. My gritty eyes made another sweep and took in a metal stand on wheels parked below an elaborately carved wooden crucifix depicting Christ in his final agony. A reminder to patients at this tiny hospital to keep their own aches and pains in perspective, I guessed.

"Has anyone come looking for me?"

Brother Fay's two-thousand-megawatt smile dimmed. His baby face didn't project solemn very well, but I could tell he was giving it his best shot.

"Three men have come here."

"Who? And here, where?"

He answered in reverse order. "You are in the village of Tapigua. Miguel Samos found you. In the branches of a mesquite." His voice took on a note of wonder. "Miguel thinks at first he sees an angel."

My mother would have choked on that. Even I came darn close. Neither of us have ever considered me the least beatific.

"Miguel untangles you," Brother Fay continued, "and brings you to me."

"And you brought me to the doctor?"

"No, no. I treat you. I am physician to my small flock as well as priest."

He was a priest *and* a doctor?

Permit me a small aside here. I have nothing against overachievers. I work with three every day. Four, if you count Sergeant Cassidy's bone-deep devotion to physical fitness. For some reason, though, this twentysomething doctor/priest hit a nerve.

Maybe because I'd recently chalked up the big three-oh and all I could list on my resume were a string of car-hopping and waitressing jobs, a brief marriage, and twentysomething months as an Air Force lieutenant. Try comparing that to med school and Holy Orders.

"You said three men came looking for me," I prompted. "Did they identify themselves?"

"Two were *Policia Federal*." Brother Fay's face clouded. "I know these two. They take money and turn a blind eye to many bad things. I did not tell them Miguel had found you. Nor did anyone else in the village. We decide to hide your presence until you recover enough to tell us who you are and why these bad men search for you."

"My name is Samantha Spade. I'm a lieutenant in the United States Air Force. I was abducted by a slime named Rafael Mendoza."

The padre's breath hissed out. "He is evil, that one."

"Very," I agreed.

"We think . . . We could not prove it to the *policia*, but we believe Mendoza's men are the ones who took little Angelina. She is but nine years old when she disappears. Her parents weep and pray for her still."

The very real possibility little Angelina was now in a brothel on the other side of the border curled my hands into helpless claws.

"Why does Mendoza abduct you?" Brother Alfonz wanted to know.

"To exact revenge against a friend of mine." I didn't go into detail. I was more interested in finding out who else had come looking for me. "Who was the third man?"

"I do not know him, nor does anyone else in the village. But he offers much money to anyone who will tell him of the whereabouts of a *Norteamericana* lieutenant."

"Did he give you his name?"

"Hector Rodriguez."

No help there. He could have been a Mendoza hireling or one of Mitch's associates from either side of the border. I took my lower lip between my teeth, wincing when enamel scraped raw flesh, and tried another approach.

"How long have I been here in, uh . . . ?"

"Tapigua."

"In Tapigua?"

"Miguel finds you three days ago. You have the concussion, I think."

"You *think*?"

My opinion of his accomplishments dropped several notches.

"I could not do X-ray. Our machine breaks months ago. So I leave you to sleep and cure yourself."

"Thanks," I said dubiously.

"*De nada*. If you feel strong enough to eat, I will summon Elena. She and her daughters have tended to you these days and nights."

I'd like to tell you I didn't really care who had tended to me. I'd like to, but I can't. Doctor or not, the mere thought of baby-faced Friar Fay emptying my bedpan or tugging my hospital gown over my bare thighs made me distinctly uncomfortable.

"First things first," I told him. "What I need right now is . . ."

A deep-throated bong interrupted me. Father Doctor Alfonz smiled at my startled expression.

"That is La Grande. The largest of our bells. You will hear La Mediana next."

Head cocked, he listened with obvious delight to a second, mellower dong.

"What's with . . . ?"

"Wait." He held up a finger. "Now La Bonita. She is the smallest and had the prettiest sound until she cracks."

I contained my impatience while Bonita did her thing. She clanged three times, sounding flat even to my untrained ears. La Grande and La Mediana joined in for a final chorus. Wincing, I waited for the echoes to fade to ask.

"What's with the bells?"

"It is Sunday morning. They summon the people of Tapigua to Mass."

Sunday? I tried to remember what day Pipe Guy and pal had snatched me. Thursday, I thought. I'd spent the rest of that day in Mendoza'a guest cell and escaped in the middle of the night. That tracked with Friar Fay's assertion that I'd been at his clinic for three days.

I don't know why reconstructing the timeline gave me a panicky feeling. Probably because of the blank spaces I couldn't fill in. What happened after my frantic call to Mitch? Had he assembled a task force? Tracked Mendoza to his hilltop lair? Gone in with guns blazing?

Or had he tried to follow my trail? Was he looking for me, along with Mendoza and this Hector Whoever.

"I need to make a call," I said urgently. "Do you have a cell phone?"

"No. Tapigua is too remote for such service. There is

a phone in my office," he added, "but I do not think you are strong enough yet to get out of bed."

"I have to."

Wrong answer. I didn't realize *how* wrong until I shoved aside the sheet covering my lower extremities and swung my legs over the side of the bed.

My bare feet thumped the floor. My hospital gown bunched around my hips. Father Fay's round, worried face blurred.

"You must eat and regain your strength," he said when I sank back against the pillows. "Tell me the name and number of the person you wish to contact and I will make the call for you."

My dizziness subsiding, I waited while he fished a pen and crumpled envelope from the back pocket of his jeans.

"Call Special Agent Jeff Mitchell." I gave him Mitch's cell phone number. "If for some reason he doesn't answer, call the Isleta office of the U.S. Customs and Border Patrol in El Paso."

I couldn't remember that number.

"Tell whoever you speak to where I am and ask them to give Special Agent Mitchell the message. Make sure they understand this is urgent. Do you have that, Father? Er, Brother?"

"*Si*. Special Agent Mitchell, Isleta office of U.S. Customs and Border Patrol."

I thought about asking him to contact one of my team members. Their numbers I could remember, but I didn't have much confidence any of them would answer. Fridays and Saturdays Dennis competes in round-the-clock online chess tournaments, so he always sleeps past noon on Sundays. Pen attends a nondenominational service before junketing off to one meeting or another. Sergeant Cassidy clanks away on his Universal Gym and probably wouldn't hear the phone. Rocky . . . Okay, I don't know what Rocky normally does on Sunday mornings. I'm not sure I really want to.

"Please, let me know if you get hold of Special Agent Mitchell."

"*Si, si*. And I will send Elena and her daughter to tend you."

Crumpled envelope in hand, he hurried out. I had barely settled against my pillows when he hurried back in with two people hard on his heels. One was a woman in a dark dress and white, bib-like apron with a large bottle clutched in white-knuckled hands. The other was a giant.

I kid you not! The man stood at least six-eight, with shoulders so broad he had to turn sideways to get through the narrow door. If Tapigua boasted a village tailor, this guy undoubtedly kept him in business. No way he could have bought his starched white shirt and Sunday-go-to-Mass suit off the rack.

"This is Elena," Father Fay said, worry stamped on his chubby face. "And Raoul. He tells me strangers approach. They bring an evil-looking dog that sniffs the trail."

"The *policia*?"

"One wears a uniform of some sort. The others do not."

I wanted desperately to believe the one in uniform

was Mitch but couldn't take the chance. Friar Fay agreed with my assessment.

"We must hide you until we know who these people are and what they want. Raoul will carry you to the bell tower. They will not search for you there."

"Their dog will."

"Not if Elena washes away your scent with antiseptic. We must hurry now. Let Raoul lift you."

He was a gentle giant, I'll say that much for him. I'm not exactly a lightweight, but he hefted me easily and precipitated only a minor shaft of pain. Unfortunately, he wasn't particularly attentive to little things like gaping hospital gowns. Elena clucked and twitched the gown over my exposed posterior but it flapped open again as Raoul followed Friar Fay out of the clinic.

I got my first glimpse of Tapigua from the giant's arms. It sat on a low ridge, with an unimpeded view of the desert surrounding it. The village itself reminded me instantly of Dry Springs. Same dozen or so crumbling adobe houses. Same dirt road bisecting the town. Only instead of Pancho's bar/cafe/motel/convenience store, the heart of this community appeared to be its church.

I'm not Catholic, but I've spent enough time in the Southwest to appreciate the artistry that goes into even the smallest of these local churches. Tapigua's was no exception. Its adobe exterior had been painted deep ochre, the window and door frames a brilliant turquoise. A gloriously ornate stone facade decorated the front entrance. A Virgin Mary in bloodred robes smiled benignly down from a niche above the double wooden doors.

The bell tower was entered from inside the church. The very crowded church. It was crammed with villagers in their Sunday best, every one of whom slewed around in their pews and no doubt got an eyeful when the giant carted me into the vestibule.

"Raoul will carry you up the stairs," Brother Fay told me hurriedly. "I will change into my vestments and meet these men with the dog at the door. I'll stop them if they try to enter the church."

He spun off to the right. When Raoul went left, something long and snaky slithered across my shoulder. I smothered a screech and jerked away. Not a wise move with my head aching, but relief preempted pain when I identified the snaky thing as one of the bell ropes.

There were three of them, each thick and fat and shiny from long use, with faded signs on the wall behind identifying their associated bells. As Raoul maneuvered me up a set of twisting wooden steps I sincerely hoped no one would latch on to one of those ropes and set off La Grande or La Bonita.

We got stuck after the third or fourth turn. The tower had narrowed. Raoul's shoulders hadn't. Grunting, he wedged sideways in the confined space but couldn't climb any higher with me in his arms. I got an elbow loose and pantomimed for him to put me down.

"It's okay. I'll take it from here."

I wiggled out of his hold. Not am easy trick in that narrow space but I got both feet under me with only minimal damage.

"*Gracias*, Raoul."

Nodding, he backed down step by slow step. When he disappeared around a turn, I craned my neck and guesstimated the remaining stairs to the wooden platform above my head. Ten? Twelve?

I could make it.

I hoped.

The first two steps I took upright, reaching one hand behind me to keep my gown from opening and exposing my tender bottom to the rough adobe wall. By the fourth or fifth, my jaw had locked. By the eight, I was on all fours with the gown bunched around my waist to keep it out of the way.

I crawled onto the platform, panting. Sweat dripped into my eyes. Incipient nausea churned in my empty belly. I stayed on my hands and knees, head hanging and hair dragging the dusty floor, until the nausea went away. Only then did I lift my head and survey the cramped space I shared with three monster bronze bells.

Please, God, do not *let anyone grab one of those ropes!*

I'd said a lot of prayers in the past few days, I realized as I inched around La Mediana. Been helped by some good people. Sooner or later, I needed to pay it all forward.

With that thought in mind, I scooted over to the low wall encircling the platform and dragged myself up enough to peer over the rim. I couldn't see much at first. The sun was too bright, the glare too fierce.

I narrowed my eyes to a tight squint. The first object I spotted was a huge, flat, purplish mound some ten or fifteen miles away. Mendoza's mesa? It had to be!

My stomach knotted. I hadn't gotten very far in my desperate trek through the desert.

Gulping, I dragged my gaze from the distant mound and scanned Tapigua's main street in both directions. Nothing moved. Not a donkey or a goat or a chicken scratching in the sun. Nor did I see any sign of movement among the brown furrows of the recently planted cornfield outside the village. Even the scarecrow in ragged white pants and a straw sombrero drooped in the hot sun.

I didn't spot the search party until I'd crawled to the opposite side of the tower and inched my head above the wall. My heart almost jumped out of my chest when I saw them trudging up the sloping ridge. Six, no seven of them, trailed by two slow-moving vehicles. They were too far away to make out the features shaded by their hat brims.

I didn't have to! I would recognize Pen's sturdy figure, Sergeant Cassidy's muscled-up torso, and Mitch's long-legged stride anywhere! And that had to be Dennis's frizzy orange hair sticking out from under the rim of a pith helmet.

After an initial leap of joy, fear almost crushed my chest. Mitch and my gang were out in the open, plainly visible to any of Mendoza's troops that might be searching the area. They could be ambushed, be tracked by snipers, get caught in a deadly crossfire.

Reason reasserted itself in the next instant. Mitch was no dummy. He wouldn't lead a search party into danger, especially unarmed amateurs like the members of FST-3. He had to have neutralized the threat.

Motivated by the image of Mendoza's face smashed to a bloody pulp, I scuttled around La Grande and thrust my feet through the opening in the platform. I couldn't trust my legs so I went down the steps on my rear. I picked up some splinters on the way but didn't care. I was oblivious to everything but the need to get out of the tower and throw my arms around whatever team member I reached first.

Brother Fay must have heard my shout. He and Raoul and several other villagers came rushing down the aisle and met me as I hit the bottom step. As promised, the friar had pulled on a white dress and one of those priest-y things. You know what I mean. The two-sided vestment that goes over the head and drapes to the knees, with an embroidered gold cross on the front. His round face screwed up with worry as he reached out a hand to steady me.

"What is it? Why do you shout?"

"The people who are coming!" I gasped, remembering to preserve my modesty as I made for the door. "They're my friends."

Despite my surge of adrenaline-fed joy, I covered only a few yards before I stopped dead. Disbelief gave way to stunned amazement, then to a wave of hysterical delight. I plopped down in the middle of the dirt street, laughing my head off, and held out my arms.

Snoopy chugged up the rutted road ahead of the team. His glued-on plastic ears dragged the dust. His wire tail bobbed. Sensing a preprogrammed snack, he picked up speed on his toy-tractor wheels and aimed right for me.

His claw rose out of his back. His circuits hummed. Looking like a cross between a computerized shoebox and a mechanized tarantula, he humped over my outstretched leg and crawled up my chest into my arms.

CHAPTER FIFTEEN

FOR sheer glee, nothing tops a noisy reunion involving assorted friends and coworkers laughing and hugging and trying manfully not to cry while embracing each other in the middle of a one-street Mexican village with dozens of goggle-eyed townspeople looking on.

Mitch reached me first. Well, second after Snoopy. He detached the omnivorous little critter from my shoulder and tossed him aside. With that obstruction out of the way, he hauled me up and into his arms. I hung there, locked joyfully against his body, while we traded breathless questions.

"Are you all right?"

"How did you find me?"

"Did that bastard Mendoza touch you?"

"Tell me you nailed him!"

We interspersed the questions with kisses until Mitch

finally raked back my tangled hair and gave a more detailed report.

"No, we didn't get Mendoza. He was gone when we hit the mesa. We found the Hummer shortly after noon, but lost your trail there. We've been scouring a fifty-mile radius for the past three days. Didn't pick up your trail until last night."

Sounded as though I'd dusted up quite a storm with the creosote branches. I felt pretty proud of my puny efforts as the others crowded around.

"That's when Mitch contacted us," Dennis O'Reilly put in, his orange hair raining sweat beneath his pith helmet. "He wanted to know if we could program Snoopy to sniff out a very specific food source."

"Me?"

"You," Pen confirmed with a smile.

She'd dressed for the desert, I noted. Sensible boots, snug jeans, a long-sleeved blouse, and a floppy-brimmed explorer's hat with a back flap to cover her neck and straps that tied under her chin.

"All we had to do was extract the scents embedded in the fabric of the name tape, separate your distinctive identifiers, feed them into Snoopy's computers, haul him down to the wrecked Hummer. He took it from there."

"That's all, huh?"

I knew darn well the process couldn't have been as easy as Pen made it sound. Rocky's haggard appearance validated that.

Poor Rocky. He wasn't built for desert search parties. His eyes were more red than white. His face showed a pasty shade of chalk and his chest heaved under the green U.S. Border Patrol blouse that Mitch had draped tentlike over his head and shoulders.

Sergeant Cassidy, of course, had barely raised a sweat. His boots sported layers of dust and his cheeks bristled with whiskers, but he otherwise looked strong and tough and un-weathered as he hunkered down to give the wide-eyed kids a demonstration of Snoopy's skills.

Shrieks erupted as Snoop Dog zoomed toward a little girl with a big white ribbon in her hair before abruptly changing direction and taking off after an eight- or nine-year-old in a white pants and shirt and bolo string tie. The boy danced away, arms flapping as he led Snoopy on a merry chase, and Brother Fay pushed through the hubbub.

"These are your friends, yes?"

"Most definitely!" Safe and warm within the circle of Mitch's arms, I made the intros. "Guys, this is Father Doctor Alfonz. He patched me up when Miguel Samos plucked me out of tree and brought me to Tapigua."

I could see them struggling to process the titles and names and tree bit but pressed ahead.

"And this is Elena."

Practically the entire village had crowded around us now, as curious about the odd-looking strangers in their midst as my team was about them. Particularly the giant who wedged into the circle. Eyes narrowed, Mitch looked him up and down.

"This is Raoul," I explained hastily. "He's one of the good guys."

"Nice to know," Mitch muttered. He surveyed the chaotic scene and picked Father Alfonz as the one in charge. "We need to get Samantha out of the sun and hear her whole story. Is there somewhere we can sit and talk?"

"Best to carry her back to the clinic. She has not yet fully regained her strength."

Mitch swept an arm under my knees, hefted me against his dusty chest, and followed while the priest led the way to his one-room medical facility. I caught the looks my team exchanged when they noted the cracked ceiling, paucity of beds, and ancient X-ray machine gathering dust in the corner.

"Brother Doctor Alfonz and his staff are a little short on equipment," I explained as Mitch sat me on the edge of a bed, "but long on compassion. They kept my presence a secret until I recovered enough to tell them who I am."

"Her uniform says she is military," the priest offered by way of explanation. "But we don't know if she deserts from the Army or is lost in the desert or becomes ill while on exercise with Mexican troops."

His round face lost some of its boyishness.

"Then two *policia* come searching for her," he related. "We know these two. They work for Rafael Mendoza. He is evil, that one."

"You won't get any argument from us on that, Padre."

Mitch settled on the bed next to mine. It squeaked under his weight, but he ignored the sagging springs.

"Start at the beginning, Samantha. Tell me exactly what happened."

The rest of my team ranged on either side of him. Noel kept Snoopy tucked under one arm, for which I was extremely grateful. The voracious little critter obviously thought he'd locked onto lunch. I kept a wary eye on him as I took them from the snatch outside the donut shop to my lunch with Mendoza to my escape into the night.

"I owe you big time for that business with the signal booster," I told Rocky. "Worked like a charm."

He puffed up and lost some of his pasty white.

"I owe you, too, Brother Alfonz. And the people of Tapigua. I don't know how to thank you for all you've done for me."

"It is enough if you have rid us of Mendoza." He turned an anxious face to Mitch. "He is gone, yes?"

"The house on the mesa was deserted when our task forces swooped down on it. Looks like he and friends moved out in a hurry."

The priest made the sign of the cross. "Pray God they do not return."

"We also raided his Mexico City residence. Or rather, one of my associates and a squad of Mexican counter-parts did."

"Paul Donati?" I asked, all too well aware of how much Mitch must have wanted to be in on that raid.

He nodded. "They burst in on Mendoza splashing around in his pool with his wife and kids."

"Oooh, boy," I murmured. "Bet Teresa Baby loved that."

"Who?"

"Mendoza's girlfriend-slash-administrative assistant. What happened?"

"Paul says they took Mendoza in and leaned on him. Hard. But without you or a single witnesses to corroborate that he orchestrated your abduction, they couldn't hold him."

"What about the nametag? Didn't that link him to the kidnapping?"

"The tag was left on my doorstep in a sealed envelope. No prints, no DNA."

"We're almost certain we lifted Mendoza's scent from the fabric," Rocky explained, "but without a valid sample to compare it to, we can't say with one hundred percent assurance."

"There was no note?"

"Just one typed line," Mitch replied. "'Vengeance was slow in coming but would be sweet,'" he quoted.

Mendoza wasn't the only one out for vengeance. I had a score to settle now, too.

"Did Paul by any chance lean on Teresa?" I asked.

"The girlfriend?"

"Right. Slender, dark haired, with—excuse the expression, Father—*puta* shoes."

Mitch blinked at the description and shook his head. "I'm sure he did, but she must not have had anything significant to contribute."

"The hell she doesn't! Call him. Find out where she is now. In the meantime, Father, could I trouble you for my uniform? I need to get dressed."

"You have not regained your strength! You must eat and rest."

"Maybe Elena could roll up some tortillas to go. Where are my clothes?"

He looked dubious but gestured to a row of rickety metal lockers leaning against the far wall. Dennis O'Reilly opened the first to reveal a pitifully small supply of bandages and tape. The second contained pillows, blankets, and bedsheets. The third held stacks of paper-wrapped slippers and folded peek-a-boo hospital gowns like the one I was wearing. The last locker, thankfully, disgorged my ABUs and boots.

The guys, secular and otherwise, departed long enough for Pen to divest me of my gown and dress me in the under- and outerwear Elena had thoughtfully laundered.

I felt a little dizzy and had to sit down while Pen dragged a comb through my hair and tied it back in a loose braid. The dizziness passed after a moment. The pain in my temple subsided, too. The thrill of seeing Mitch and my team had spurred a near-miraculous recovery. That, and the heaping platters of rice and carne asada Elena insisted we all devour before we departed Tapigua.

My belly full for the first time in what felt like a week, I was ready to roll. Unfortunately, the break for lunch had given Mitch time to reflect.

"I want you to go back to El Paso with the team," he told me once we'd said our good-byes to Brother Doctor. "I've got a chopper standing by. I'll call it in and join Paul in Mexico City. We'll take it from here."

"I'm in this as much as you are now."

"Be reasonable, Samantha. Your testimony is all we need to prove Mendoza held you against your will. You don't need to be in on the takedown."

"Yes, I do. This is bigger than me, Mitch. Much bigger. The folks here in Tapigua lost a little girl. Father Alfonz is convinced she got sucked into Mendoza's vicious flesh-peddling schemes. You had to put Jenny out of your life because of him. If I can talk to Teresa Slut Shoes, away from Mendoza, I think I can get to her expose the entire operation."

"Think?"

"It's worth a shot."

GUESS I don't need to tell you Donati was less than enthusiastic when Mitch contacted him via cell phone and relayed my request for a personal heart-to-heart with Mendoza's girlfriend. I couldn't really blame Paul for his explosive reply. The two other cases I'd worked with him had turned nasty. Not *totally* my fault, I hasten to add, but these FBI types have convenient memories.

"Ask him where Mendoza is now," I hissed at Mitch, who duly voiced the question.

"Some big charity do," he relayed. "Evidently it's been planned for months."

"Ask him . . ."

"Here." He thrust the phone at me. "You ask him."

"Paul, it's Samantha."

"Glad Mitch found you in one piece, Lieutenant."

Ever wonder how some people can inject so many nuances into a single sentence? This one contained genuine sincerity, weary resignation, and more than a touch of "Please! Go home and let us do our thing."

"Thanks."

Wish I could convey the same wealth of emotions

with minimal expression. Guess I need to work on my delivery.

"Listen, Paul, we can crack Mendoza."

"We?"

"He's got an Achilles toe."

"Heel," Mitch corrected dryly.

"Heel. In this case, the heel's name is Teresa."

"Teresa Sandoval? His assistant?"

"You think so, huh?"

Paul gave a huff of reluctant laughter. "Yeah, we got the impression she might provide Mendoza more than administrative services."

"Did you interview her?"

"Of course."

"Did she admit being with her boss on the mesa?"

"She did."

"And?"

"She saw nothing, heard nothing."

"Did you play the wife card?"

There was a short, telling silence. "Not with her," Donati admitted after a moment. "We tried it on Mendoza, though. He just smiled and said his wife understands that a man must be a man."

Teresa hadn't found the situation nearly as amusing. I'd almost gotten whiplash when I asked her about Mrs. Boss.

"I want to talk to her, Paul. Can you and your friends get to her? Discreetly detach her from her boss so we girls can have a heart-to-heart? We need to do it fast, though. Before Teresa has time to think about what she knows and doesn't know."

"Hang on."

I waited impatiently while he conversed in hurried Spanish with someone on his team. I heard a second person bark an order, waited a few moments more, and got my answer.

"She's at the same function the Mendozas are attending. Taking bids on the piece he put up for auction."

Perfect! The boss makes her work while he schmoozes with his wife. Teresa Baby had to be steaming.

"Mitch says he can call in a chopper. We'll be there in less than an hour."

IF you think L.A. collects smog, try choppering into Mexico City sometime. One minute you're skimming above an impenetrable layer of brown goop. The next, you're nose-diving in and hoping to hell it dissipates before you hit the ground. Or in this case, before you hit the ramparts of a massive stone castle with four lethal towers poking into the sky.

I'd visited Chapultepec Castle before, when O'Reilly was invited to compete in the opening round of the Chess Tournament of the Americas. He'd talked Pen and me into taking leave and tagging along as his personal cheering section. We sat for five long, boring hours while Dennis and his competitor shuffled pieces across a board. He lost in the first round, thank heavens, so we spent the rest of the weekend hitting bars, pyramids, and at Pen's adamant insistence, a museum or two.

One of those museums was located at the base of Chapultepec Castle. But the rock it sat on looked a *lot* higher and steeper than I remembered from our brief visit. Especially when the chopper pilot swooped around a turret and aimed for the black-and-white-tiled piazza at the rear of the castle.

The rectangular piazza jutted out above heavily wooded grounds. I spotted a string of limos, at least four of which were heavily armored and guarded by uniformed personnel. Their plates were obscured for security reasons but I glimpsed a subdued U.S. flag shoulder patch on one of the uniformed guards standing at parade rest.

"Mitch! Are those U.S. Marines?"

He squinted and nodded. "Embassy guards. Evidently the guest list includes the U.S. ambassador as well as the mayor and governor."

Ooooh, boy. A U.S. ambassador, a governor, and a mayor. I hoped to heck gate-crashing their big wingding didn't come back to bite me in the ass. I would have enough to explain to Dr. J without the State Department and a foreign government coming down on me.

Paul's counterpart had obviously cleared us in. A police officer in a bright orange vest waved us to a pad near the ramp that led up to the castle gate.

"You want to ease up a bit there, Samantha?"

"What? Oh!"

I loosened the nails I'd gouged into Mitch's thigh, then dug them right in again as the landing pad zoomed up at us. He merely grunted and, once the skids had touched down, pried my hand loose.

Paul had sent a car and driver to pick us up. I took great reassurance from the sight of those U.S. Marines as Mitch and I zinged past the parked limos and drove up onto the castle ramparts.

Most of the security personnel ringing the walls wore camouflage fatigues like mine, desert greens like Mitch's, or the spiffy all-black of the governor's personal bodyguards. I half expected one of those razor-jawed blackshirts to challenge us, but Paul Donati was waiting to thrust us through a side door into a small anteroom.

"Couldn't talk her out of it, could you?" he commented to Mitch in disgust.

"You had your shot, Donati. I didn't notice you doing better."

"Yeah, but she's your woman."

I knew darn well Donati said that to get a rise out of me but I actually kind of liked the way it sounded.

"Enough man talk," I interjected sternly. "Where's Teresa?"

"Inside."

He nudged me toward the door of the anteroom. It gave onto what looked like the castle's main reception hall. A vaulted ceiling soared fifty or more feet in the air. Fluted stone pillars marched at regular intervals down a marble-tiled hall at least two football fields long. Works of art occupied spotlit niches between the pillars. Including, I saw with a catch to my breath, the magnificent eagle dancer that had recently graced the foyer of Mendoza's cliff house.

Teresa stood beside the sculpture, lean and sensuous in a black sheath slit to the knee on one side. I couldn't see her shoes, but there was no missing the scarlet, come-and-get-me hibiscus tucked in the knot of her hair. Or her intense concentration as she followed the movements of a couple across the room.

Rafael Mendoza, I saw with a sudden spike in my pulse. With a languid blonde at least three inches taller than him on his arm. Diamonds dripped from her ears and sparkled in the choker that ringed her neck.

My glance zinged back to Teresa. She was doing a damned good job of hiding her feelings, but I was betting on the fact that they were simmering just below the surface. I poked Paul in the ribs.

"Send someone to get her. We'll wait out on the piazza."

"You sure you know what you're doing?" Mitch asked when we'd moved to one of the parapets that overlooked acres of green below.

"No. Just play along, okay?"

AFTER all my furious thinking and plotting, Teresa fell apart at the seams the first moment she saw me.

"They said . . ." She stumbled back and put up a hand as if to ward off a ghost. "They said you wrecked the Hummer . . . That you wandered into the desert on foot. They said you could not survive."

"They said wrong."

"How did you . . . ? Where did you . . . ?"

"Never mind me. Let's talk about your boss."

As shaken as she was, she recognized that we were after bigger game and made a painfully obvious effort to pull herself together.

"I don't know why Señor Mendoza brought you to

the mesa. He never told me the reason, only that . . ."
She wet her lips and glanced nervously from me to
Mitch to Paul and back to me again. "Only that I must
make sure you were treated well while you were there."

"Bull!"

"I swear!"

"And I suppose he never told why he'd had ringbolts
soldered to the flooring of the plane that ferried me in.
And ferried out terrified little girls and boys."

"I don't know what you're talking about."

Her nostrils flared. She backed up another step. Two.
I followed relentlessly.

"You don't know about a girl named Angelina?"

"No! No, I never hear of her!"

"Then I'll tell you about her. She comes from the
village of Tapigua. She went missing last year. Her
parents and the parish priest believe one of Mendoza's
squads picked her up and sold her to a brothel. She
wouldn't have brought much in the way of profit. Not
enough to pay for the diamonds your boss likes to drape
all over his wife."

That slipped in under her guard. She stiffened and
flashed me an evil look but held her own.

"I say again, I don't know this girl or . . ."

"Listen to me!" I cut in ruthlessly. "Your boss is going down, Teresa, and not just for kidnapping me. You're
going with him. Unless you decide he's used you long
enough and want some payback."

"He does not . . ." She stopped, frowned, continued
a little less adamantly. "He does not use me."

"No? When's the last time he danced with you in

214

public? Or invited you to join him and his family for a splash in the pool?"

That was laying it on pretty thick, but I was on a roll.

"You think your lover's going to protect you when I get on the stand and identify you as one of his cohorts? Not hardly! If Mendoza runs true to form, he'll try to eliminate me . . . and anyone who can verify the truth of my story."

"I . . . I . . ."

Mitch stepped forward then. His face might have been carved from the same stone as the castle walls.

"Your lover's done it before," he said in a tone so low and lethal I felt goose bumps crawl up my arms. "Four years ago he went on trial right here in Mexico City. I testified at that trial. So did my counterpart on the task force. Ramon's son disappeared a week later. I made sure Mendoza couldn't get to my daughter, so he took Samantha instead. He would have killed her, Teresa. Slowly and painfully. The same way he'll kill anyone he considers a threat."

"Better watch your back," I advised her cheerfully. "Or let these guys watch it for you."

CHAPTER SIXTEEN

THE scariest moments of my whole south-of-the-border sojourn came just after Paul and his pals donned vests emblazoned with various official insignia and invaded the charity auction. They marched up to Mendoza and cuffed him right in front of the ambassador, the governor, the mayor, and his wife.

She threw a first-class, scream-your-lungs out, claw-everyone-within-reach hissy fit. I don't know all that many Spanish four-letter words, but Señora Mendoza added considerably to my repertoire. It took three men to subdue her while two others escorted her husband down the colonnaded hall and out onto the piazza.

Mendoza didn't put up any resistance. No doubt because he was already mentally figuring which judges he could pay off and how many jurors he would have to intimidate.

Then he spotted me.

And Mitch.

I don't know what he said to Mitch. All I can say is that it had a real nasty ring to it.

I *do* know what Mitch said in reply. I won't repeat it here. Suffice to say Mendoza's response forever shattered my faith in handcuffs as a means of restraint.

Like an enraged bull, he shook off the men holding him, lowered his head, and charged. He moved so fast that Mitch barely had time to shove me aside before taking a head butt to his midsection.

No big deal ordinarily. You gasp for air. Toss up the carne asada you had for lunch. Kick the crap out of the buttee. Go on about your business. Except when you're six-one or -two and standing close to a low stone wall!

Mendoza had hit so hard and fast that Mitch toppled backward. I had an instant, terrifying vision of him flying over the wall and crashing into the woods below. My heart in my throat, I lunged forward to try to catch him.

I could have saved my panic and my effort. Mitch had already regained his balance. He swatted me aside, brought his knee up, and smashed it into Mendoza's groin.

The Mexican screamed in agony and doubled over. His legs gave out. He started to crumple, but before he dropped, Mitch grabbed his collar.

"That was for Ramon's son. And this, you worthless piece of shit, is for Samantha."

The knee slammed into his face this time. Bone crunched. Blood spurted. I whooped with glee.

Mendoza fell to the tiles, writhing in agony. I know it's very uncool to hit a handcuffed man while he's down. Probably against the Geneva Convention, too, but I was in no mood for nice. Hauling back my left foot, I gave him a good, solid combat boot to the gut.

"And that, buddy boy, is for Angelina and all the others like her."

I know, I know! Not a smart move. With a governor, a mayor, an ambassador, and a host of media looking on, yet. Given Mendoza's penchant for beating every charge brought against him, I figured I would find myself on the losing end of an assault rap before long. Can't say I cared.

NATURALLY the melee at the castle was the lead story on every Mexico City TV station that night. It also made the front page of the dailies the next morning. Not that I had either the linguistic ability or the time to read them. Paul hauled Mitch and me downtown at the crack of dawn so I could give my statement to at least a half dozen different investigative agencies.

Representatives from several more were lined up at the door when Mitch worked some kind of magic and won a reprieve. We caught a U.S. Border Patrol flight back to El Paso late Monday afternoon. He also arranged for the Cessna C550 Citation to land unannounced at a small private airport.

Although I was in no way, shape, or form up for another media barrage, I owed Junior Reporter a huge favor for broadcasting that interview with Rocky. As whipped as I was, I decided to repay it by granting him an exclusive.

He met us at the airport, so eager for the interview he tripped over the camera equipment twice when positioning for the interview. His crew eventually got him planted and his mike adjusted.

"Is it true . . . ?"

"Hang on a sec." I stepped over the cables and straightened the collar of his pale yellow shirt. "That's better. You were saying?"

"Is it true you were abducted by Rafael Mendoza, the Mexico City magnate who allegedly heads an international human smuggling organization?"

I could tell he expected my standard no comment. Or a referral to the Fort Bliss Public Affairs office. Even getting that much on camera would be a coup. So he almost dropped his mike when I answered forcefully.

"Nothing alleged about it. The guy traffics in young boys and girls."

"You, uh, got proof of that?"

"Oh, yeah!"

Teresa Baby had spilled her guts. Was still spilling them when Mitch and I departed Mexico. Acting as Mendoza's administrative assistant had given her access to all kinds of paper and electronic files.

The paper trail showed that Mendoza's hirelings were equal opportunity kidnappers. They'd snatched children on both sides of the border as well as several young girls visiting with their families from Europe. Interpol was involved now, as were a host of different agencies from Mexico, the U.S., and Canada. Mendoza wouldn't buy or terrorize his way out of this one.

His other operations were collapsing right and left,

too. U.S. and Mexican SWAT teams had already conducted several lightning raids. Mitch got a call that they'd filled a warehouse with drugs and contraband that included guns, cigarettes, and pirated electronics.

Unfortunately, I couldn't share all these delicious details with Cub Reporter until Paul Donati and company gave me the green light. I could, however, expound on the role Mitch, my team, and Snoopy played in my rescue.

And DeWayne himself. He blushed and stammered when I mentioned his interview with Rocky.

"I, uh, didn't understand one word in three Dr. Balboa said."

"That's okay; I did." More or less. "And I'm very pleased to report that the experimental Self-Nurturing Find and Identify Robot featured in your previous interview performed excellently in very rough field conditions."

I'd tipped DeWayne that I was going to mention the SNFIR. Thus his crew was ready with a photo of Snoopy to flash up for their viewing audience.

"My team and I intend to conduct additional tests under more controlled conditions," I announced to the world at large and Dr. J in particular. "But we're hopeful the military might field a prototype within months, maybe a year tops."

"Thank you, Lieutenant Spade."

The camera switched to Junior Reporter, who struggled heroically to hide his glee while remaining solemn and Tom Brokaw-ish.

"This is DeWayne Wilson, for Channel Nine News."

Mitch hid a grin as DeWayne and company packed up their gear. "You just made that kid's week, if not his year."

"I hope so. He certainly made mine when he got Rocky on camera. That's one box I can check off," I commented as we started for the Border Patrol Range Rover idling at the edge of the grassy strip.

"Box?"

"I made of list of favors I need to repay. DeWayne was on the list. Farmer Farnsworth was right behind him."

"Who?"

"Snoopy's inventor. His baby took all kinds of heat after that business with the heads. I aim to set it right."

"Well, you made a good start with DeWayne."

"You're on the list, too," I commented casually. "Right at the top, as a matter of fact."

Casual got tossed out the window when he curled a knuckle and stroked it across my cheek. The look in his hazel eyes made my breath stop and my knees go rubbery.

"You don't owe me any favors, Samantha. Having you home, relatively unhurt, is all I want or need."

Great! He had to pick a moment when I was hot, sweaty, and covered with dust to turn my insides to mush. And he knew it, too!

Smiling, he gave my cheek another pass. "Let's get you home. Then we'll talk about who tops whose lists."

He stuck two fingers in his mouth, let loose with a whistle that just about drilled through my eardrums, and signaled the driver of the Range Rover.

* * *

MY three-room apartment couldn't compare to Mendoza's high desert mansion in either spaciousness or tidiness. The usual clutter had acquired a layer of dust. Newspapers and an assortment of glamour mags lay scattered across the floor. The coffee mug I'd deposited on the counter before leaving for work almost a week ago now sported a greenish ring around the rim. And the light on my answering machine, I saw, showed a steady, unblinking red.

"Aren't you going to check the messages?" Mitch asked as I brushed past the machine. "Or take that call?" he added as the phone began to ring as if on cue.

"Nope," I said over the strident ring. "That's either a reporter, begging for an interview, or one of my family members, praying I'm okay and hoping I'll get around to collecting my share of the reward, like, soon."

With the recorder full, the caller couldn't leave a message. Two seconds later, my cell phone rang. I let it go to voice mail.

Sure enough, it was my uncle Alex, relieved to know I was all right and wanting to know when I could help him out with that in-ground pool. Halfway through his message I switched off the cell phone and took the house phone off the hook.

"There! My loving clan can wait until tomorrow for me to tell them I've already spent the reward."

"You have?"

Surprised, Mitch looped his arms around my waist. Since we were still in the uniforms that had seen several days of hard wear, his loose embrace raised little puffs of dust.

"When did you have time to shop between getting kidnapped and kicking Mendoza in the balls?"

"You got him in the balls. I connected a few inches higher."

I leaned back in his hold, feeling warm and safe. And stupidly happy when he gave me a lazy grin.

"Mendoza's attorneys may try to make something of that," he warned.

"Let 'em. I'll sic Lawyer Nowatny on them."

"Lawyer Nowatny?"

"Oh, I forgot. You were in Seattle when my brother, Don, sent me his personal ambulance chaser. Don assured me the guy can wring blood from a stone. In fact . . ."

I pursed my lips as a new thought struck me.

"Uh-oh." Mitch hooked a brow. "I've seen that look before. What are you thinking, woman?"

"I'm thinking," I said slowly, "I might promise Lawyer Nowatny a percentage of whatever he can recover in a civil suit filed on my behalf against Mendoza. The damages should at least equal my share of the reward money."

"Which you've already spent."

"Well, no cash has changed hands yet. I have to work the details out between DARPA and the FBI and . . ." I stopped and cocked my head. "You don't know any local companies that sell or refurbish X-ray machines, do you?"

"You mean, like the devices that screen for weapons or contraband at airports?"

"No, the ones that screen for broken bones. Friar Alfonz said theirs had been out of commission for months. I figure fixing or replacing it is the least I can do for him and the others who helped me. Maybe some medical supplies, too. Their cupboards were pretty bare. Oh, and a new bell. La Bonita is cracked, or so Brother Doctor informed me."

Grinning, Mitch scooped me into his arms and headed for the bedroom. "What about Charlie? I heard through the grapevine that he's keeping a real low profile these days. Since you're in such a magnanimous mood, are you going to help him out of his jam, too?"

"I suppose," I replied with noticeably diminished enthusiasm. "He'd better not show up to collect it with Brenda the Boob in tow, though."

Laughing, Mitch bypassed the bed and made straight for the bathroom. It's not easy stripping off two sets of uniforms, boots, associated accessories, and undergarments in my tiny excuse for a bath, but we managed.

We also managed to squeeze into my three or four cubic feet of shower. Together. Mitch did the honors first, shampooing my hair and lathering up a washcloth to make sure he didn't miss an inch of me.

I won't say I melted into a puddle of mush. I came close, though. Especially when he wedged around and spread his palms against the tile so I could soap down his back, hips, and tight, trim butt.

It was his thighs that got me, though. Strong and corded and fuzzed with light gold hair. I stroked the soapy washrag down the outside of one and felt the weirdest sensation. As though this was exactly where I was supposed to be. Right here, in this tiny shower. With this man.

"Mitch?"

"Mmmm?"

"I'm pretty sure I love you."

He thought about that while I slid the washrag up, then down his other leg. I was beginning to wonder whether I should have dropped the dreaded L word when he squeezed around. Smiling, he leaned into the spray beating down on us.

"Let me know when you're a hundred percent. Like me."

"Whoa! Hang on there, big guy." I planted my fists on his chest and dodged his kiss. "When did you hit a hundred percent?"

"I don't know."

"Think! A girl likes to know these things. Was it last week, when Mendoza took me? Last month? Last year?"

"Hell, Samantha, I don't know. Might have been the first time you manhandled that EEEK contraption into my Range Rover." He raised his hands and smoothed back my streaming hair. "Just take my word for it, sweetheart. I'm there."

ONE of El Paso's rare gully washers was rattling the windows when Mitch and I rolled out of bed a little past six a.m. the next morning.

His choice, not mine. I would have snuggled for another hour or two and tried again to pinpoint exactly when he'd reached that magic one hundred mark. But his district commander wanted a report ASAP on the events down in Mexico, and conscientious trooper that he is, Mitch, made me coffee, dressed, delivered several kisses, and hit the door.

I lolled in bed, sipping my coffee, and toyed with the idea of flipping on the TV. After last night, though—and one extremely satisfactory session early this morning—I didn't want to spoil my mood with nonstop Mendoza stories.

Or with calls from importuning relatives. I left the recorder full, the house phone off the hook, and my cell phone on silent through another shower, solitary this time, followed by a final cup of coffee.

Tough, gung-ho military officers consider umbrellas a total wimp-out. I would never pop one open except under extraordinary circumstances. Covering the ten yards from my front door to my car without drowning qualified in my book.

My Sebring sat in all its dents under the carport. Someone—Noel I guessed—had arranged to have the taillights fixed during my absence. I called a silent blessing down on him as I pulled away from the carport's protective shield.

The rain pounded the streets in big, fat splats. Not a happy circumstance in a city that averages less than ten inches a year. Traffic didn't crawl. It petrified. Stuck in a river of red taillights, I drummed my nails on the wheel to the rhythm of the windshield wipers as I inched forward. Frustration as much as an on-the-spot decision to reward my troops had me pulling into the same donut shop I'd vanished from almost a week ago.

The owner of the shop spotted me through the window to the bakery part of the shop. "It's you! The lieutenant!"

Hard to deny it with subdued rank on my collar tabs. I nodded, and he flew through the swinging door, dusting his floury hands on his white apron.

"Josie! Bring a box! Give the lieutenant whatever she wants, our compliments."

"Thanks, but I can't acccpt gratuities."

"Gratuities, shamooities."

Having thus disposed of at least seven volumes of Department of Defense regulations, he beamed while Josie filled the box with my team's favorites and flatly refused to accept payment.

"Really, I can't accept . . ."

Inspiration struck when I spotted a tin coffee can on the counter with a taped sign indicating this establishment supported the Summer Special Olympics. I stuffed a twenty in the can to appease my conscience and whatever DOD gods might be looking over my shoulder.

I say that in jest. Now. But I can state with utter truthfulness that my heart just about popped out of my chest when I learned not twenty minutes later that I had, in fact, a very powerful DOD god coming down on me.

I got the word when I dashed through the side door, clutching a soggy donut box and my wimpy umbrella. The first person I met was Dennis. His orangey hair stood on end and his eyes were huge, almost eclipsing his nerdo black frames.

"Techno Diva! Where the hell have you been?"

The near panic in his voice made me blink. "Mexico. Remember?"

"You got home yesterday afternoon," he accused.

And yesterday was a duty day, I remembered belatedly. So I didn't call in and let the team know I was taking the rest of the day off? What was the big deal?

"I was a little tired." I injected just a touch of sarcasm into my drawl. "Being kidnapped, rolling a Hummer, whacking my head against its window, and taking down a syndicate kind of does that to me."

"Never mind the syndicate. What's wrong with your phones? We've been trying to reach you since you got home. So has Dr. J."

Eeeeuw.

"I'll call him as soon as I get squared away," I promised Dennis.

"You don't need to call him. He's here."

"Here?" I echoed faintly. "In El Paso?"

"In your office."

Double eeeeuw.

"He got in late last night. Like I said, we've been trying to reach you."

I seriously contemplated running back out into the rain, but that would only delay the inevitable. I wasn't facing Dr. J with a box of donuts, though. He'd read the gratuity guilt all over my face.

"Here." I shoved the donuts at Dennis. "Get rid of these."

It said much for the state of O'Reilly's mind that he upended the box and crammed it in a trash can. Ordinarily he would have concealed the goodies until the coast was clear.

I had my breathing more or less under control by the time I approached my office. Wish I could say the same for my nerves. I had to swipe my sweaty palm against my leg twice before offering it to my boss.

"Dr. J! So good to see you, sir."

He set aside a cup containing a pale liquid that had to be one of Pen's herbal concoctions. She was sipping one with him, as were Rocky and Sergeant Cassidy. Judging by the carefully neutral expressions on all three male faces, it wasn't their first cup.

Dr. J rose and took the hand I held out. "I was very relieved to hear you'd come through that horrible ordeal in Mexico with no serious injuries, Samantha."

"Thanks."

He assumed a stern expression. Not an easy trick for a guy in a blue and yellow polka-dot bow tie. "I would have preferred, however, to hear it from you personally."

"Yes, sir. The thing is . . ."

Ooops! Full stop. I couldn't exactly explain the thing was Mitch's thigh. Or that it was connected to other parts that had kept me humming and happy right up until the moment I walked in the door.

But I could tell him about Snoopy.

"I don't know if the team had a chance to tell you about the field performance of the Self-Nurturing Find and Identify Robot, sir. They programmed it to track me down in the middle of the desert. The little sucker can sniff out anything."

Dr. J's stern expression gave way to a gleam of genuine interest. "Drs. England and Balboa have been filling me in on its capabilities. I see great potential there, Samantha. Great potential."

Rain still hammered down outside, but inside my

office was suddenly all smiles and sunshine. This is what FST-3 was all about! This is why we put up with each other's idiosyncrasies. Why we endured all those long days out at our test site. We'd finally hit on something that might, just might, significantly improve the capability of our combat troops.

"I'm so glad you see Snoopy's possibilities, Dr. J. If you'd like, we can clear the hallway and give you a demonstration."

"Clear the hall?"

"We still have a few waterlogged computers stacked in the corridor," Sergeant Cassidy explained. "They're left over from the fire.

"Not to worry," I added hurriedly as my boss gulped and tugged on his bowtie. "They're going to computer heaven as so as I finish the paperwork."

"Yes, well . . ."

"I'll have it done this week. I promise. Barring any further visits from ex-husbands, electrical fires, or kidnappings, that is."

My feeble attempt at a joke hit like the proverbial brick. Sergeant Cassidy gazed at the ceiling, Rocky smoothed a palm down his shirt front, Dennis grimaced, and even Pen had to work to summon a smile.

"Actually," Dr J. said again, "obtaining a demonstration of, er, Snoopy's capabilities is only one of the reasons I flew out to El Paso. I wanted to assure myself that you are all right . . ."

"Awwww."

"And," he continued, fighting what looked suspiciously like a smile, "present these."

"These" I saw when he reached into his pocket, were two shiny silver bars sitting side by side in a dark blue velvet case.

"Congratulations, Lieutenant. You've completed the time in grade and met the requirements of honorable service to qualify for promotion to the rank of first lieutenant."

"You're kidding!"

His bemused expression said he sort of wished he was. But he made up for that momentary lapse with a firm shake of his head. "No, Samantha, I'm not."

My team jumped in to offer congratulations. They ran the gamut. I got a fierce hug from Pen, a hoot and high five from Dennis, an awkward back pat from Rocky, and an unintentional bone-crunch of a handshake from Noel.

"By the way," Dr. J let drop when the noise died down. "We need to make this official, so I asked the deputy post commander to assist me in pinning on your bars this afternoon."

"Colonel Roberts?" I squeaked. "You asked Iron Butt Roberts to pin me?"

"I did."

"What did he say?"

Dr. J's smile widened to a full-fledged grin above his polka-dot bowtie. "Something along the lines of 'God help the United States Air Force.'"